JAKE M
GRAPHIC

SKATEBOARD SUMMER

STONE ARCH BOOKS
a capstone imprint

JAKE MADDOX
GRAPHIC NOVELS

Published by Stone Arch Books,
an imprint of Capstone.
1710 Roe Crest Drive
North Mankato, Minnesota 56003
www.capstonepub.com

Library of Congress Cataloging-in-Publication Data
Names: Peters, Stephanie True, 1965- author. |
    San Juan, Mel Joy, illustrator. | Reed, Jaymes, letterer.
Title: Skateboard summer / text by Stephanie True Peters ;
    art by Mel Joy ; lettering by Jaymes Reed.
Description: North Mankato, Minnesota : Stone Arch
    Books, a Capstone imprint, [2021] | Series: Jake Maddox
    graphic novels | Audience: Ages 8–11.
Identifiers: LCCN 2020025186 (print) | LCCN 2020025187
    (ebook) | ISBN 9781515882336 (library binding) |
    ISBN 9781515883425 (trade paperback) | ISBN
    9781515892250 (eBook PDF)
Subjects: LCSH: Graphic novels. | CYAC: Graphic novels. |
    Skateboarding—Fiction. | Friendship—Fiction. |
    Summer—Fiction. | Camps—Fiction.
Classification: LCC PZ7.7.P44 Sk 2021 (print) | LCC
    PZ7.7.P44 (ebook) | DDC 741.5/973—dc23
LC record available at https://lccn.loc.gov/2020025186
LC ebook record available at https://lccn.loc.gov/2020025187

Summary: Sondra and her best friend, Jonathan, are heading
to the summer camp of their dreams—Camp Vert. In order to
fit in at the competitive skateboarding camp, the two friends
decide to learn a challenging new trick, the frontside 180
heelflip. When the friends' cabins compete against one another
at camp, will they both master the trick? And more importantly,
will they stay friends in the middle of the rivalry?

Editor: Aaron Sautter
Designer: Brann Garvey
Production Specialist: Tori Abraham

Printed in the United States   5442

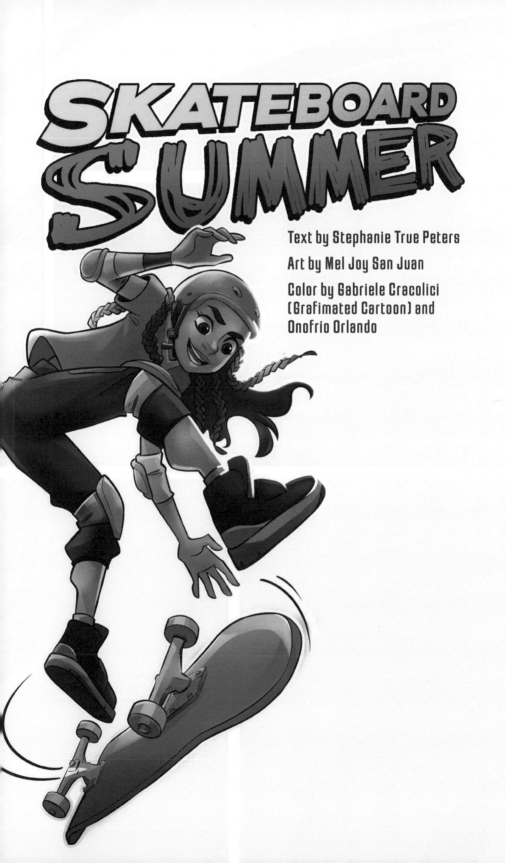

SKATEBOARD SUMMER

Text by Stephanie True Peters

Art by Mel Joy San Juan

Color by Gabriele Cracolici
(Grafimated Cartoon) and
Onofrio Orlando

STARTING LINEUP

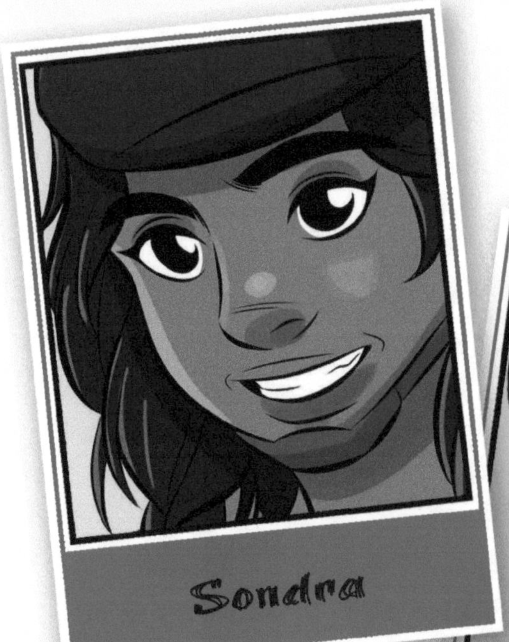
Sondra

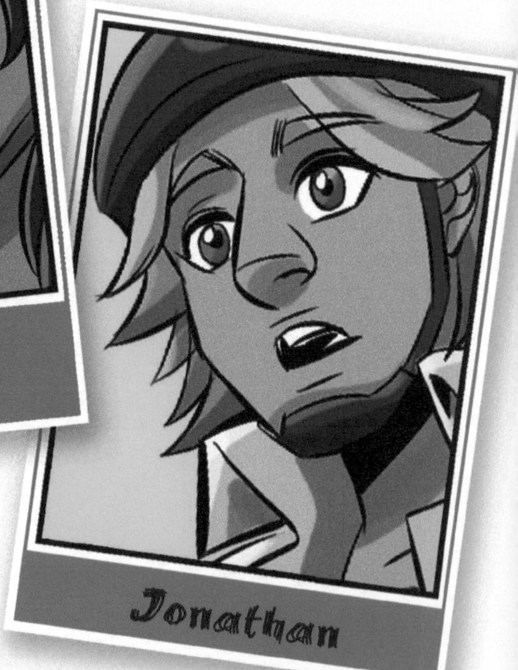
Jonathan

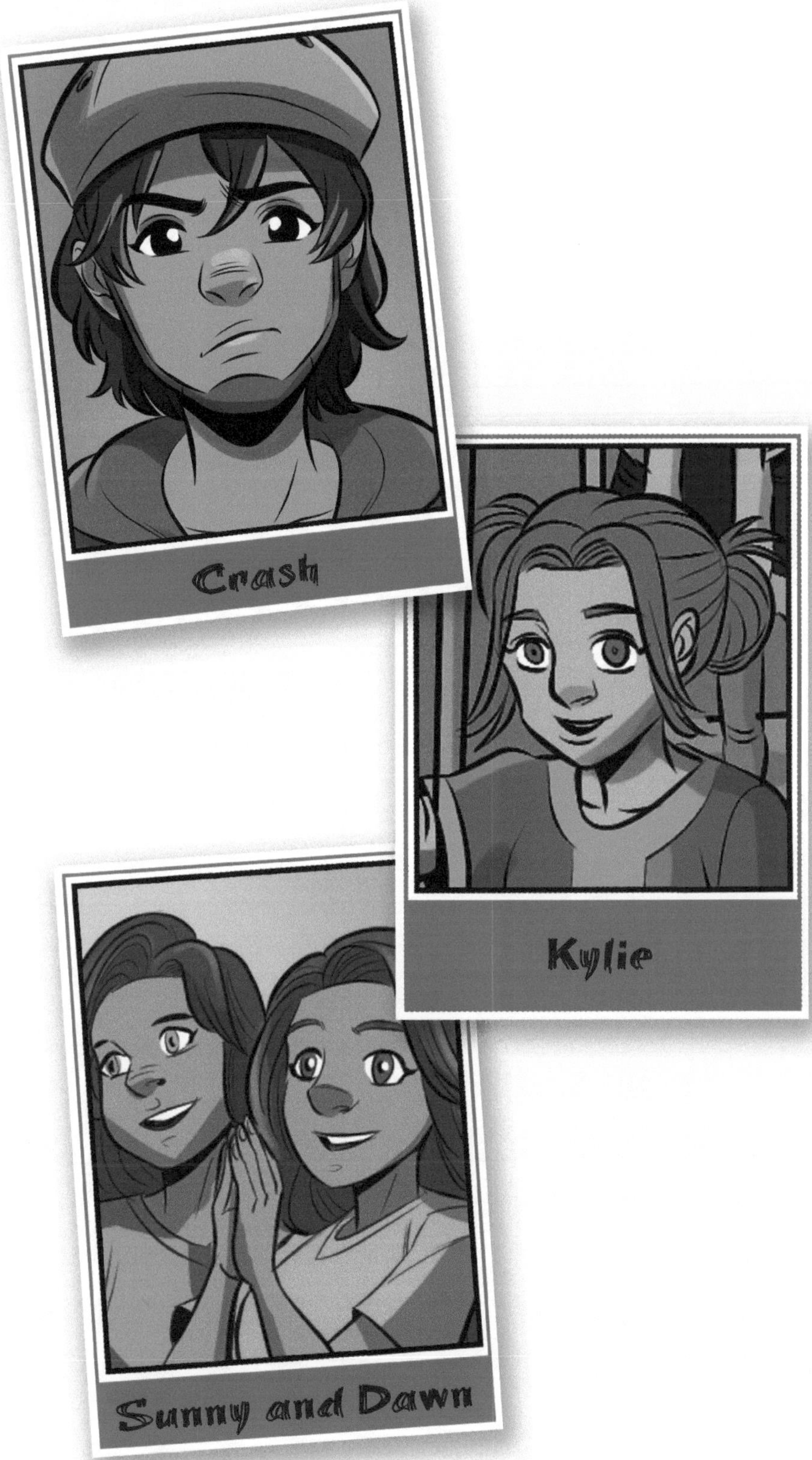
Crash
Kylie
Sunny and Dawn

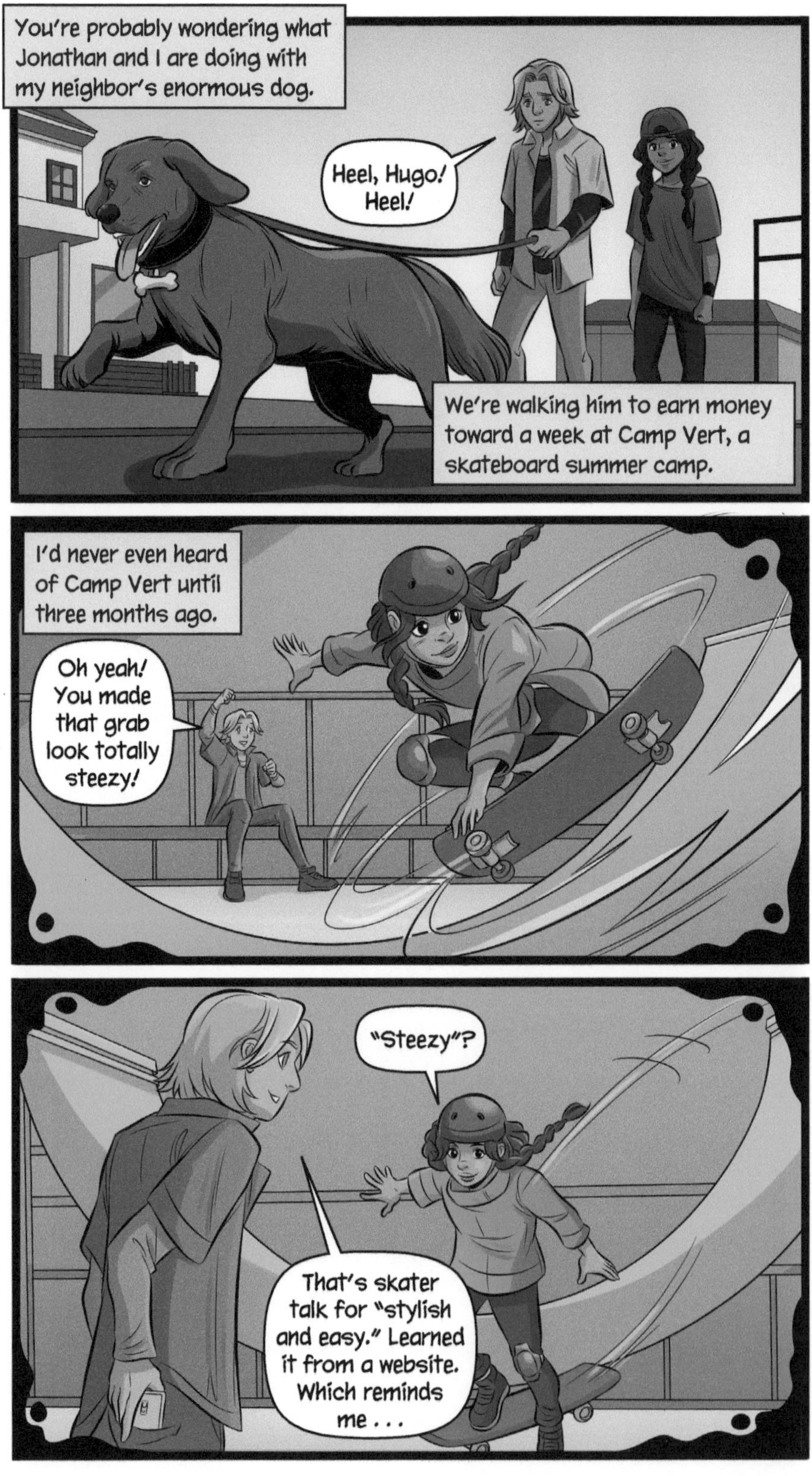
You're probably wondering what Jonathan and I are doing with my neighbor's enormous dog.
Heel, Hugo! Heel!
We're walking him to earn money toward a week at Camp Vert, a skateboard summer camp.
I'd never even heard of Camp Vert until three months ago.
Oh yeah! You made that grab look totally steezy!
"Steezy"?
That's skater talk for "stylish and easy." Learned it from a website. Which reminds me . . .

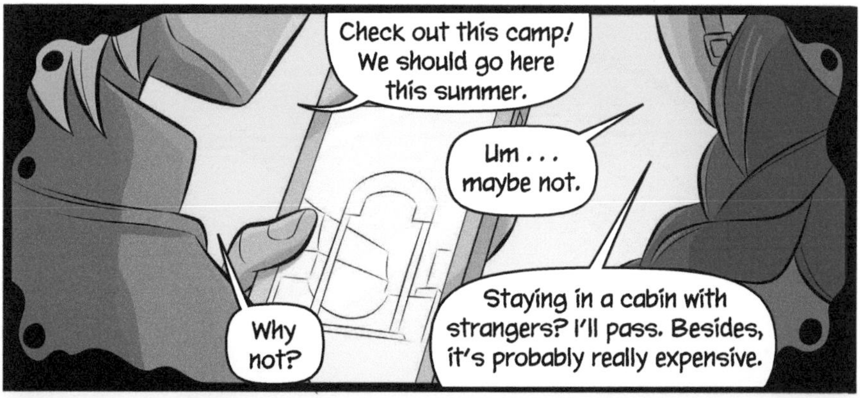
Check out this camp! We should go here this summer.
Um . . . maybe not.
Why not?
Staying in a cabin with strangers? I'll pass. Besides, it's probably really expensive.

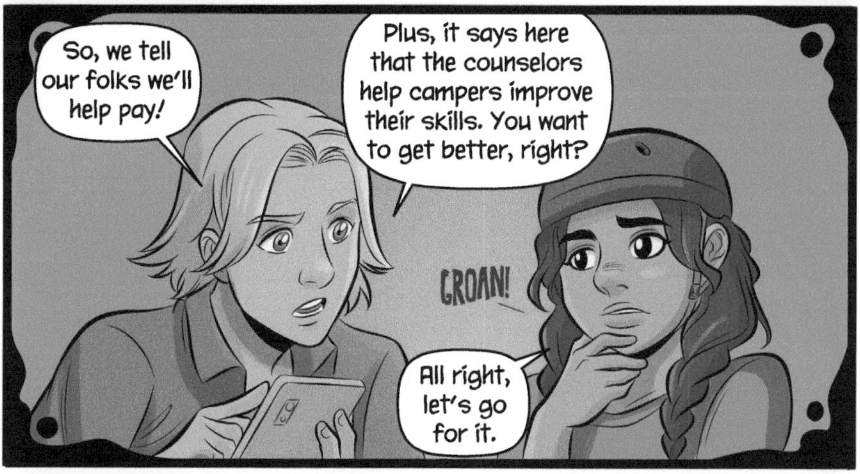
So, we tell our folks we'll help pay!
Plus, it says here that the counselors help campers improve their skills. You want to get better, right?
GROAN!
All right, let's go for it.

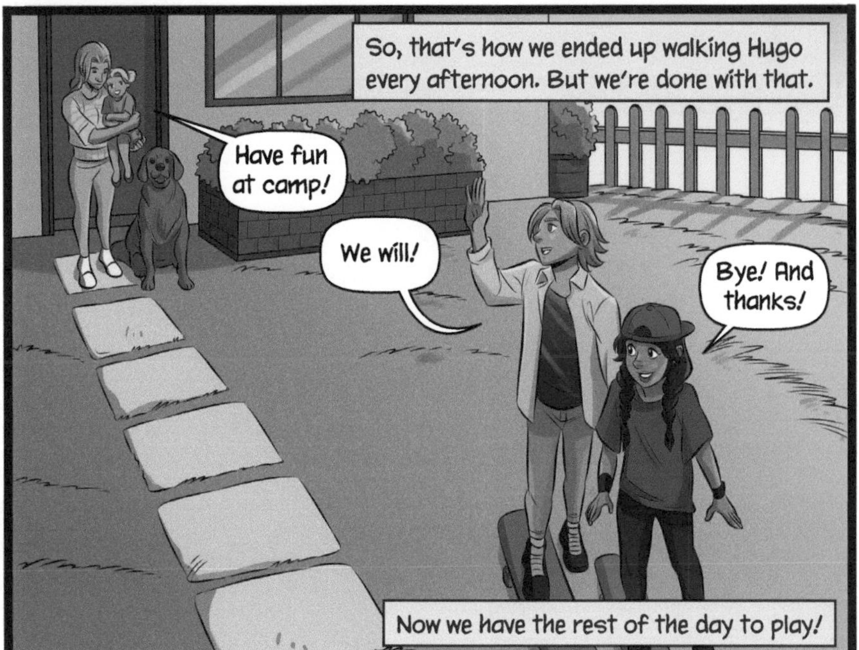
So, that's how we ended up walking Hugo every afternoon. But we're done with that.
Have fun at camp!
We will!
Bye! And thanks!
Now we have the rest of the day to play!

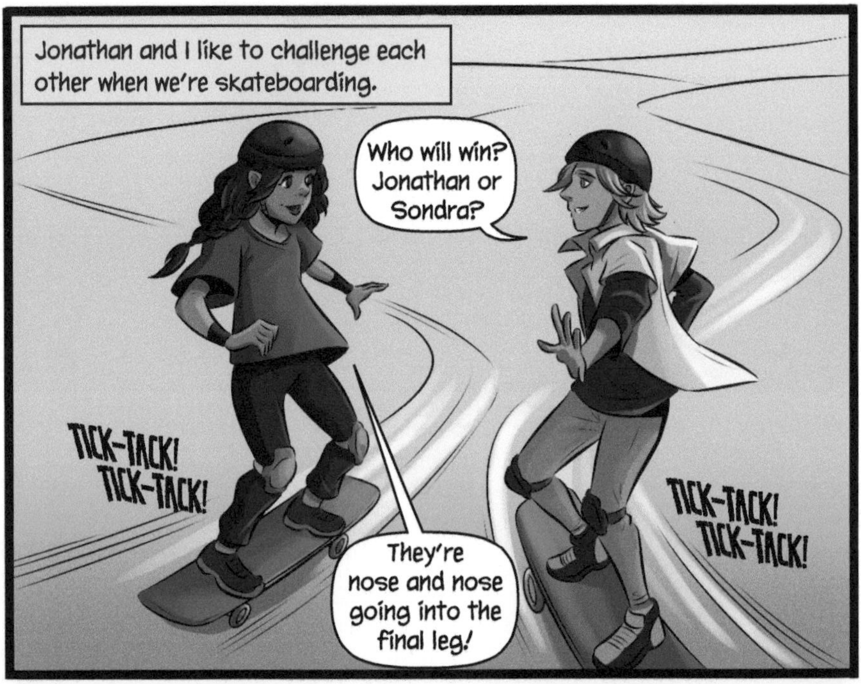
Jonathan and I like to challenge each other when we're skateboarding.
Who will win? Jonathan or Sondra?
TICK-TACK! TICK-TACK!
They're nose and nose going into the final leg!
TICK-TACK! TICK-TACK!

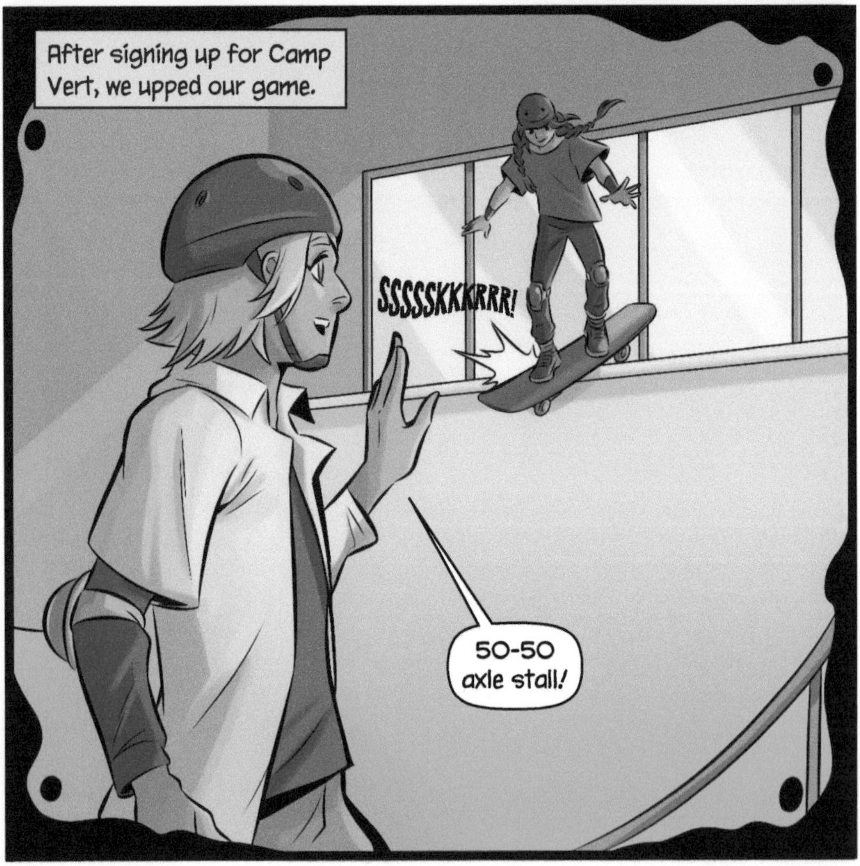
After signing up for Camp Vert, we upped our game.
SSSSSKKKRRR!
50-50 axle stall!

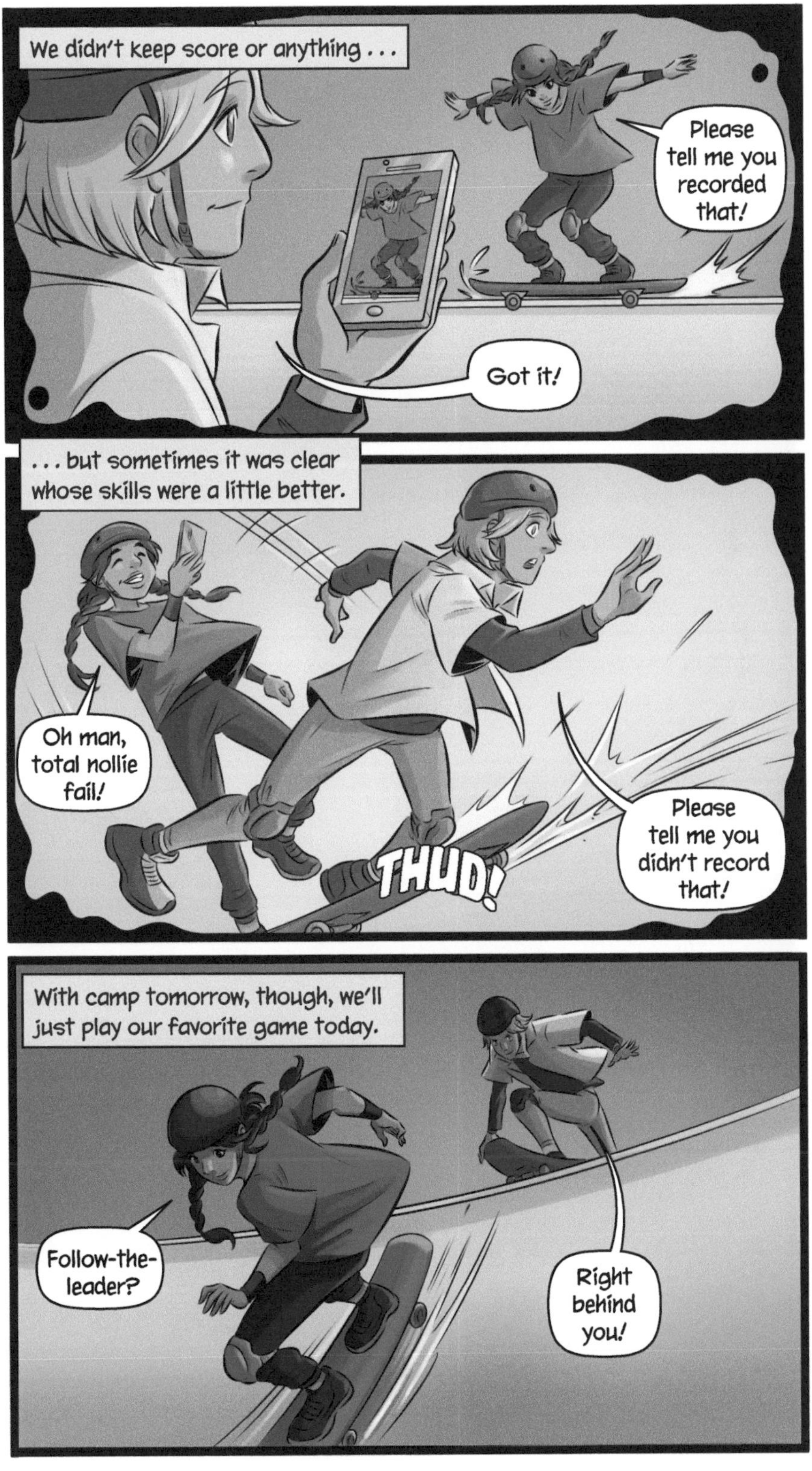
We didn't keep score or anything . . .
Please tell me you recorded that!
Got it!
. . . but sometimes it was clear whose skills were a little better.
Oh man, total nollie fail!
THUD!
Please tell me you didn't record that!
With camp tomorrow, though, we'll just play our favorite game today.
Follow-the-leader?
Right behind you!

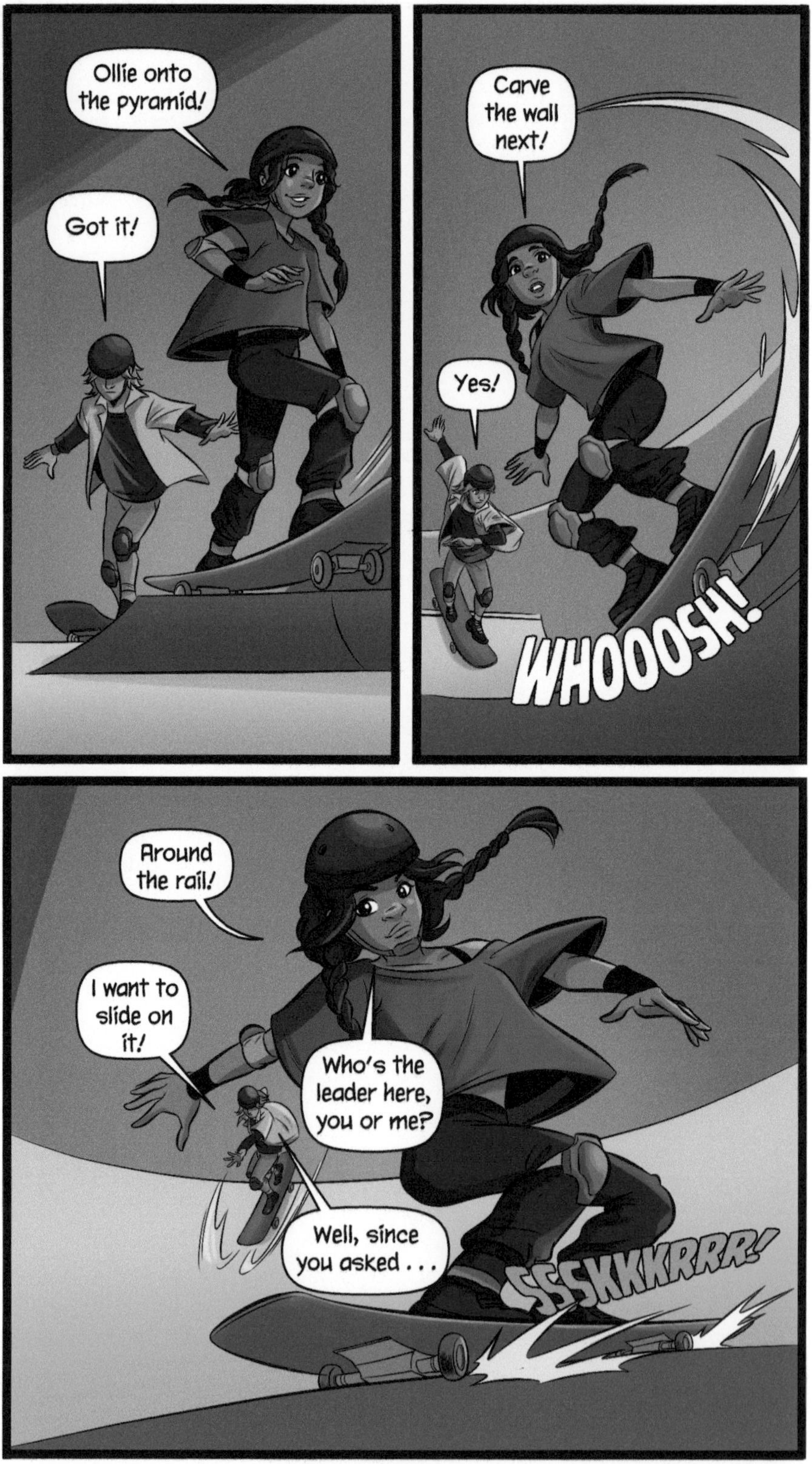
Ollie onto the pyramid!
Got it!
Carve the wall next!
Yes!
WHOOOSH!
Around the rail!
I want to slide on it!
Who's the leader here, you or me?
Well, since you asked . . .
SSSKKKRRR!

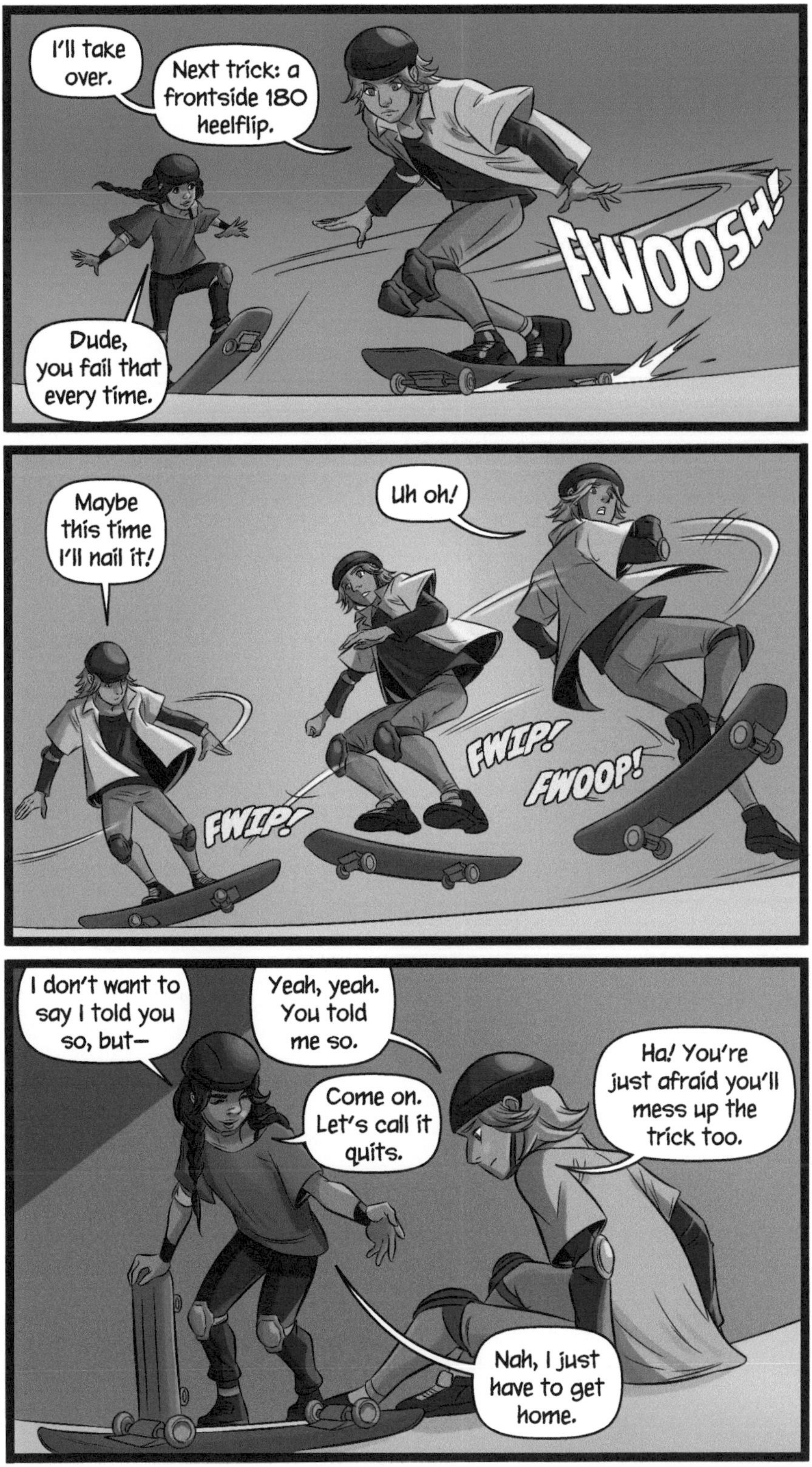
I'll take over.
Next trick: a frontside 180 heelflip.
FWOOSH!
Dude, you fail that every time.
Maybe this time I'll nail it!
Uh oh!
FWIP!
FWIP!
FWOOP!
I don't want to say I told you so, but–
Yeah, yeah. You told me so.
Come on. Let's call it quits.
Ha! You're just afraid you'll mess up the trick too.
Nah, I just have to get home.

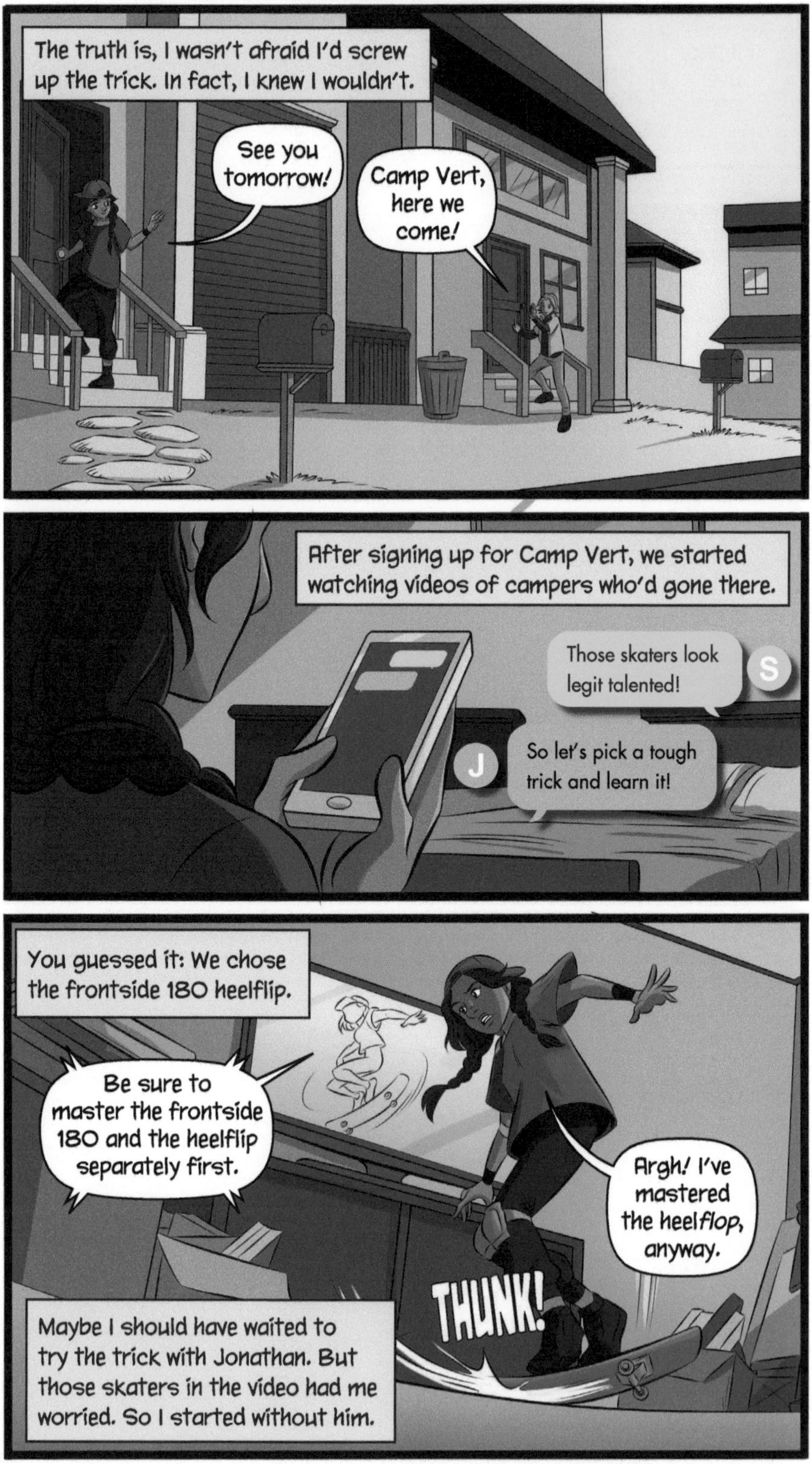
The truth is, I wasn't afraid I'd screw up the trick. In fact, I knew I wouldn't.
See you tomorrow!
Camp Vert, here we come!
After signing up for Camp Vert, we started watching videos of campers who'd gone there.
S
Those skaters look legit talented!
J
So let's pick a tough trick and learn it!
You guessed it: We chose the frontside 180 heelflip.
Be sure to master the frontside 180 and the heelflip separately first.
Argh! I've mastered the heel*flop*, anyway.
THUNK!
Maybe I should have waited to try the trick with Jonathan. But those skaters in the video had me worried. So I started without him.

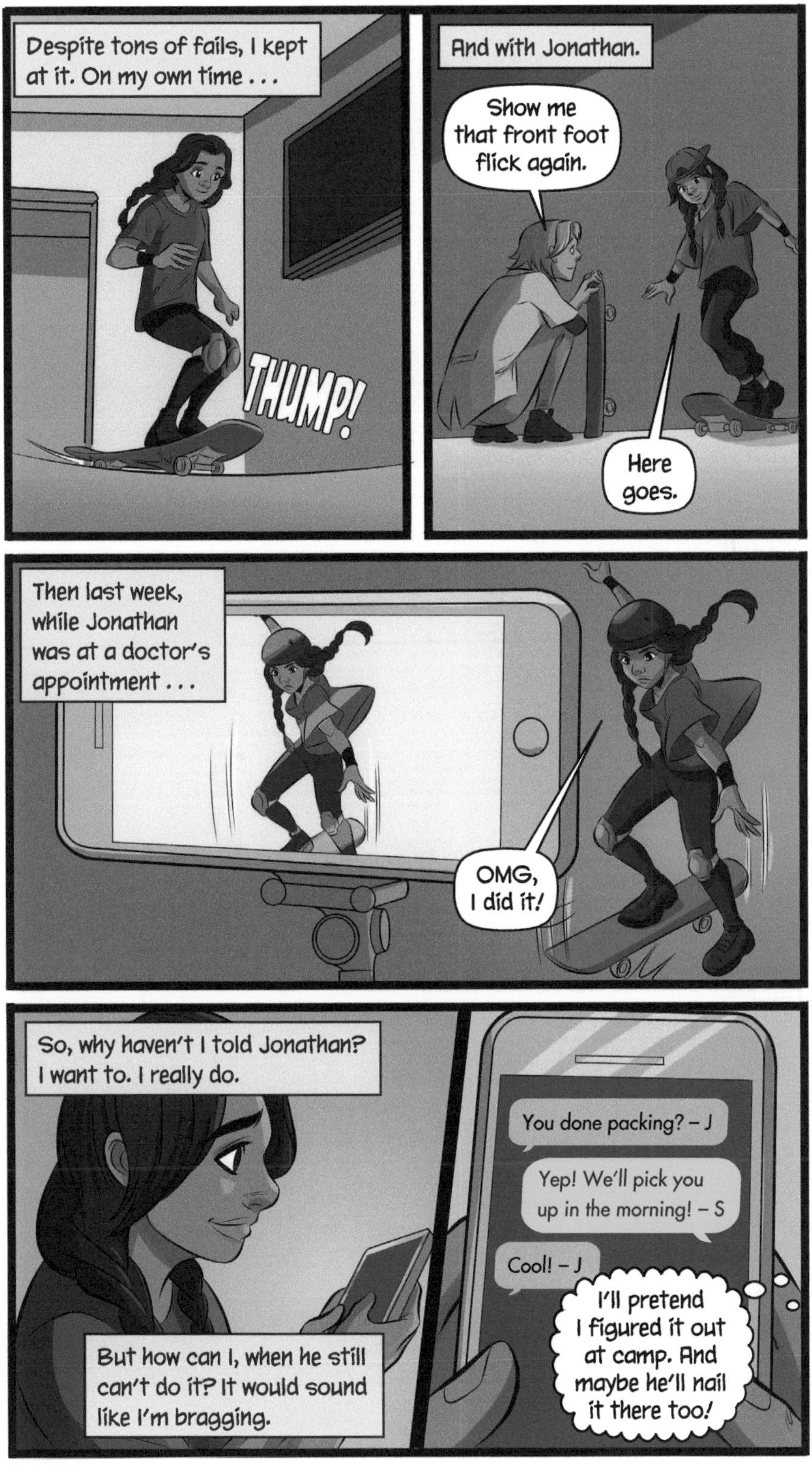

Despite tons of fails, I kept at it. On my own time . . .
THUMP!
And with Jonathan.
Show me that front foot flick again.
Here goes.
Then last week, while Jonathan was at a doctor's appointment . . .
OMG, I did it!
So, why haven't I told Jonathan? I want to. I really do.
But how can I, when he still can't do it? It would sound like I'm bragging.
You done packing? – J
Yep! We'll pick you up in the morning! – S
Cool! – J
I'll pretend I figured it out at camp. And maybe he'll nail it there too!

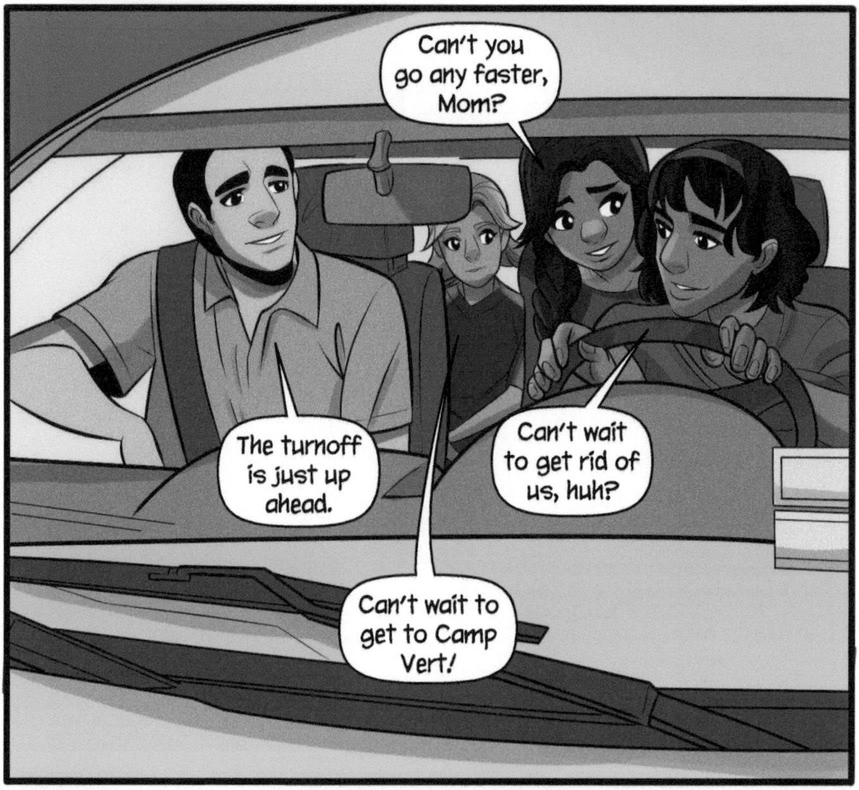
Can't you go any faster, Mom?
The turnoff is just up ahead.
Can't wait to get rid of us, huh?
Can't wait to get to Camp Vert!

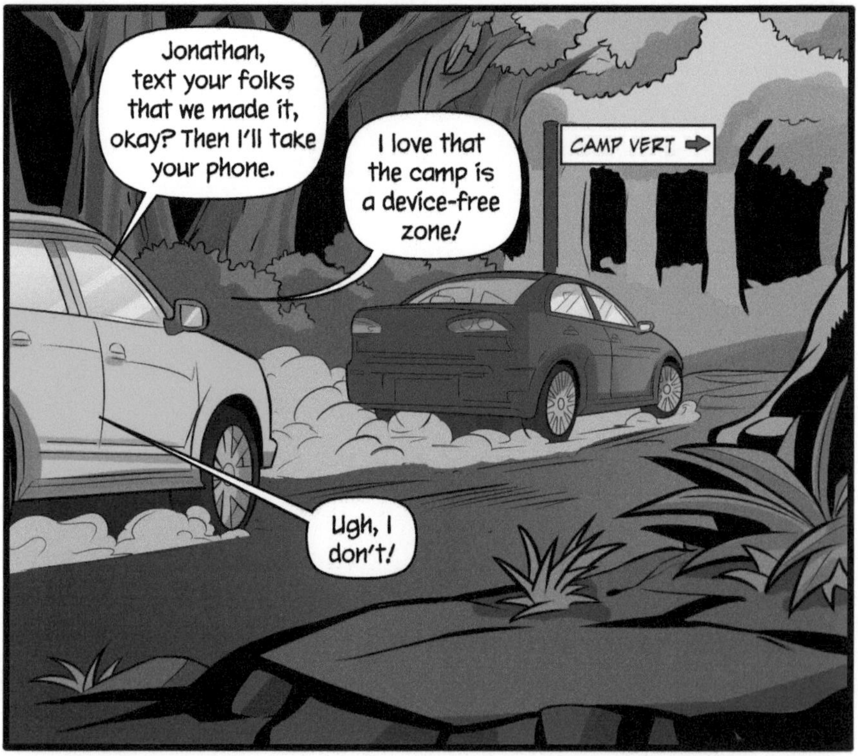
Jonathan, text your folks that we made it, okay? Then I'll take your phone.
I love that the camp is a device-free zone!
CAMP VERT
Ugh, I don't!

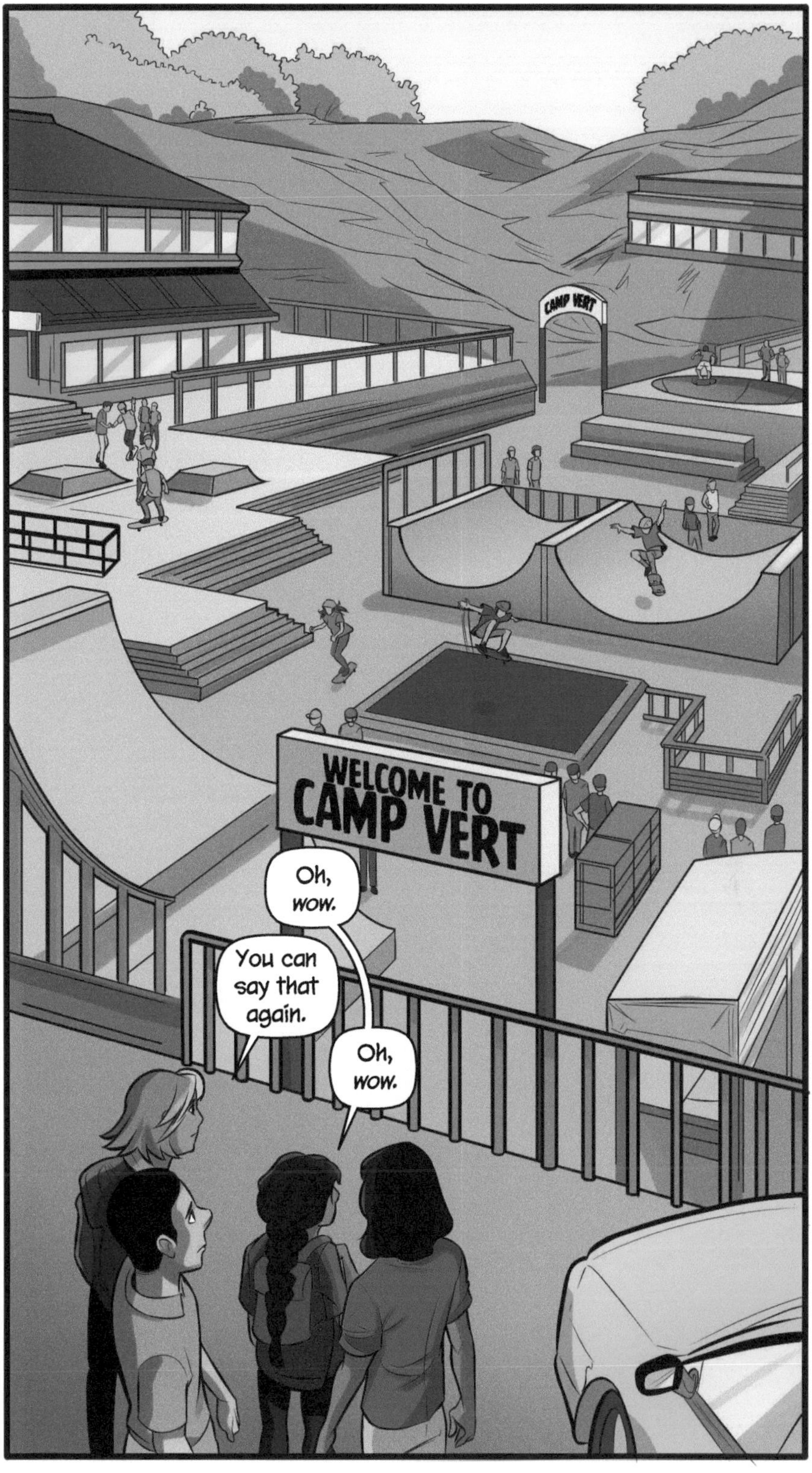
CAMP VERT
WELCOME TO CAMP VERT
Oh, wow.
You can say that again.
Oh, wow.

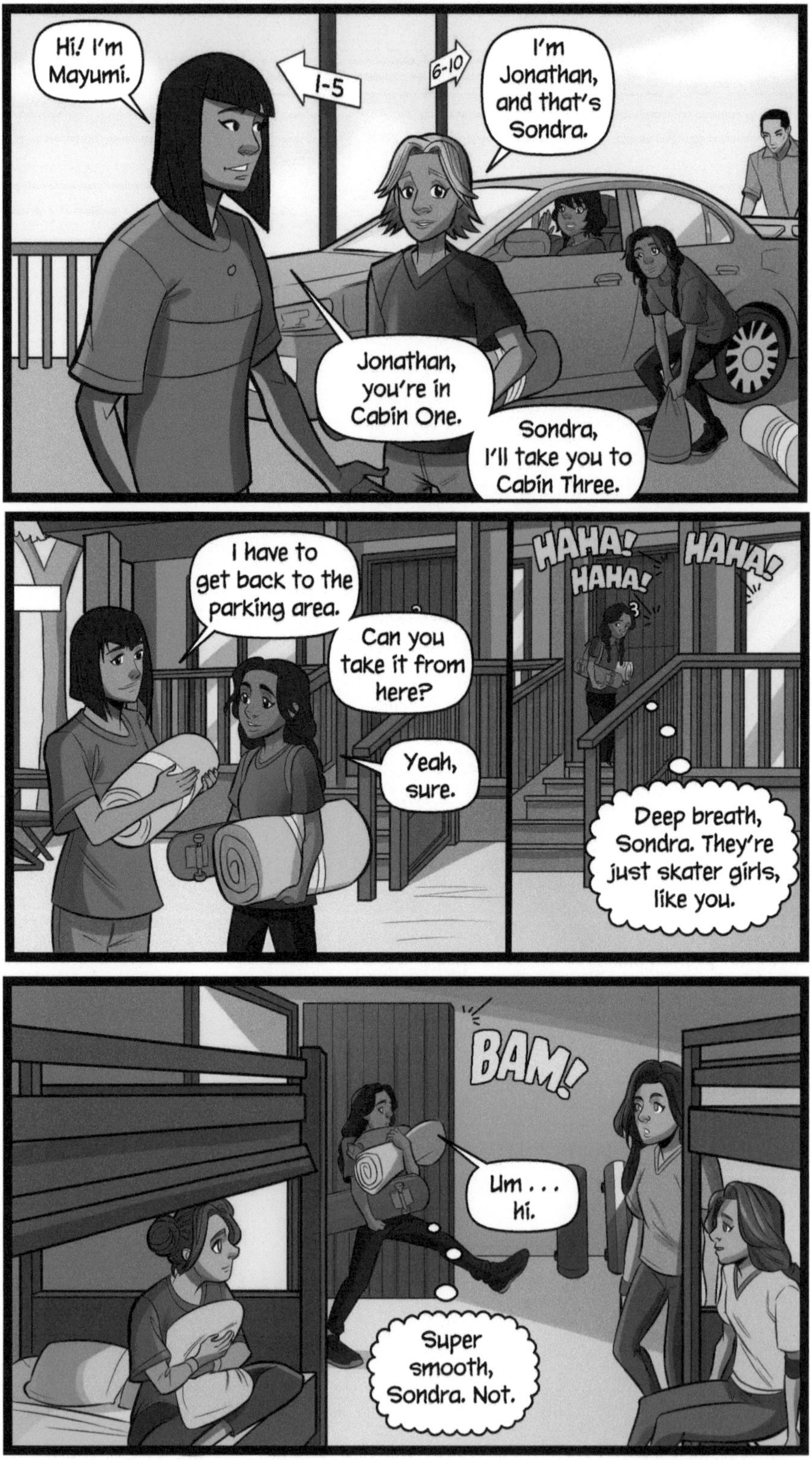

Hi! I'm Mayumi.
1-5
6-10
I'm Jonathan, and that's Sondra.
Jonathan, you're in Cabin One.
Sondra, I'll take you to Cabin Three.
I have to get back to the parking area.
Can you take it from here?
Yeah, sure.
HAHA!
HAHA!
HAHA!
3
Deep breath, Sondra. They're just skater girls, like you.
BAM!
Um . . . hi.
Super smooth, Sondra. Not.

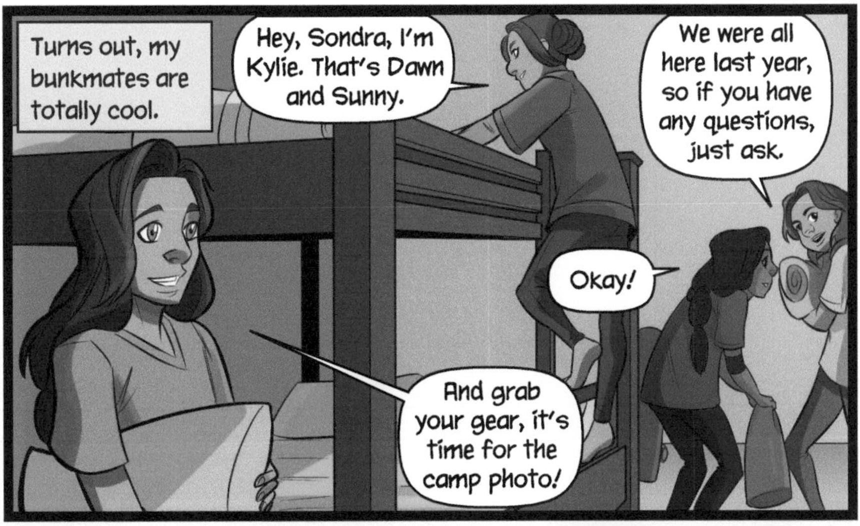
Turns out, my bunkmates are totally cool.
Hey, Sondra, I'm Kylie. That's Dawn and Sunny.
We were all here last year, so if you have any questions, just ask.
Okay!
And grab your gear, it's time for the camp photo!

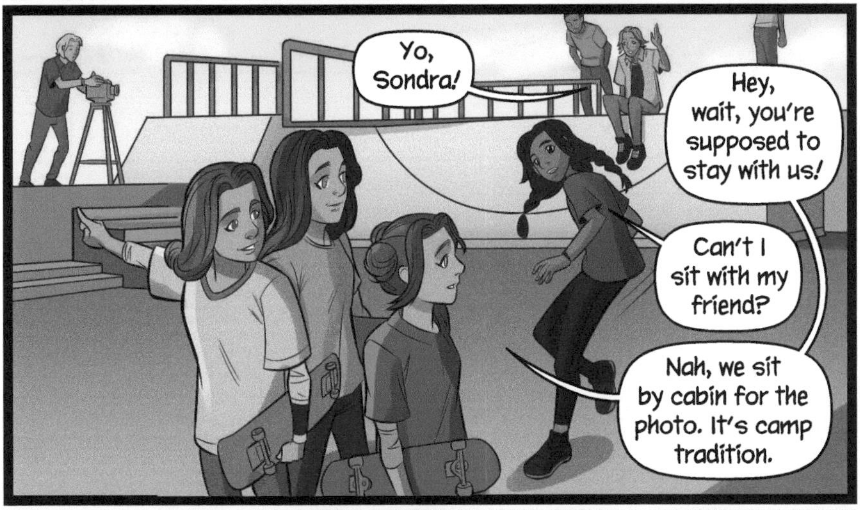
Yo, Sondra!
Hey, wait, you're supposed to stay with us!
Can't I sit with my friend?
Nah, we sit by cabin for the photo. It's camp tradition.

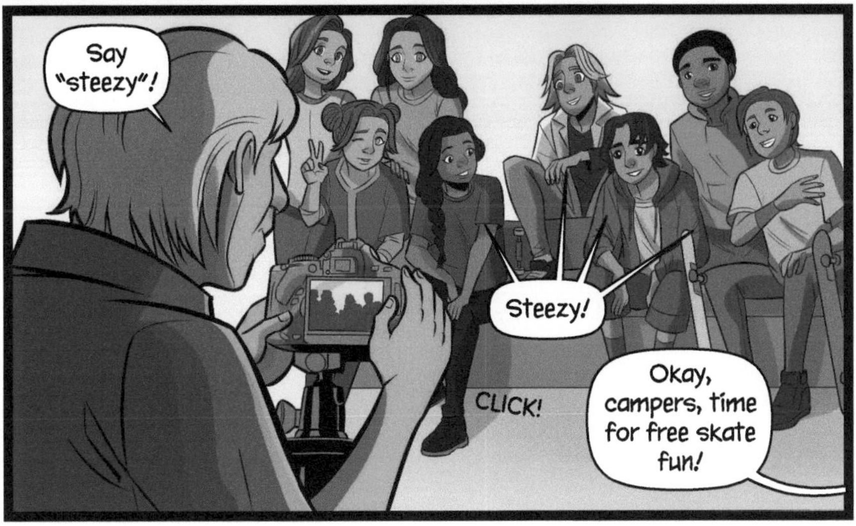
Say "steezy"!
Steezy!
CLICK!
Okay, campers, time for free skate fun!

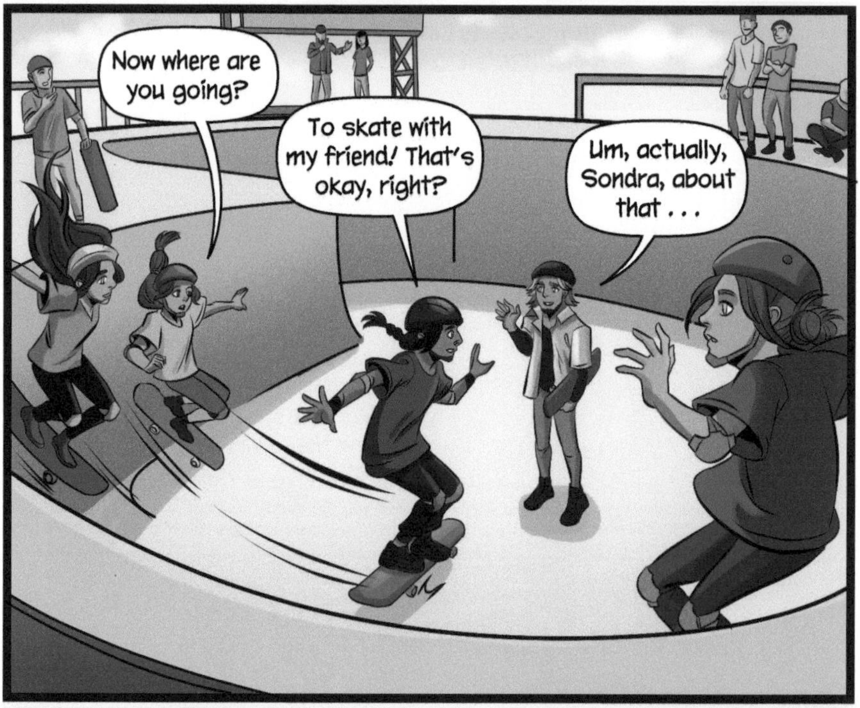
Now where are you going?
To skate with my friend! That's okay, right?
Um, actually, Sondra, about that . . .

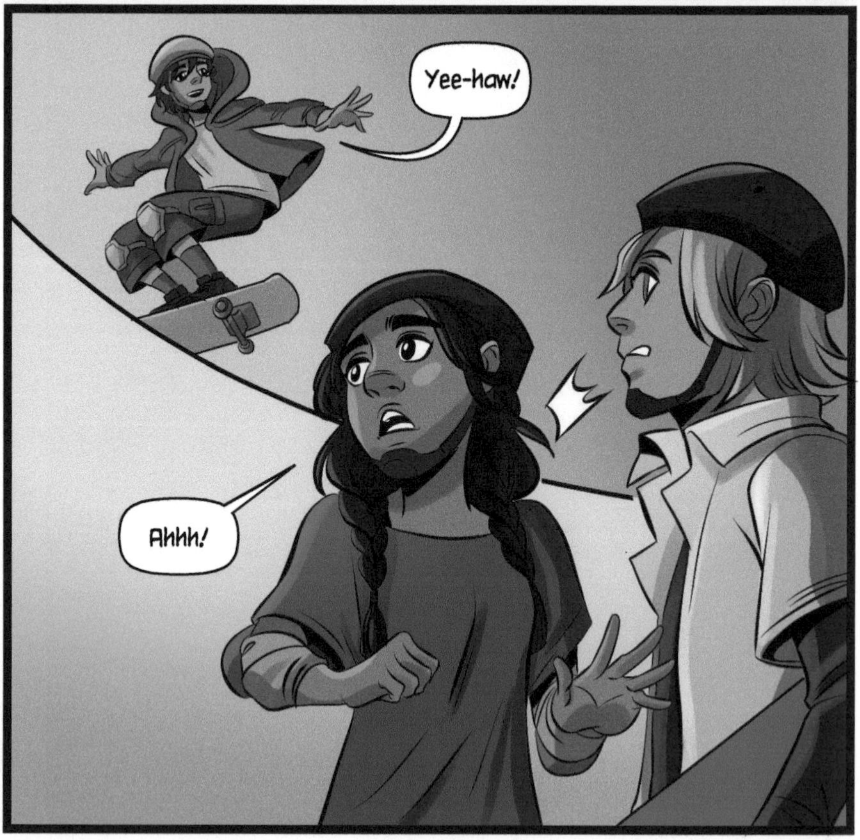
Yee-haw!
Ahhh!

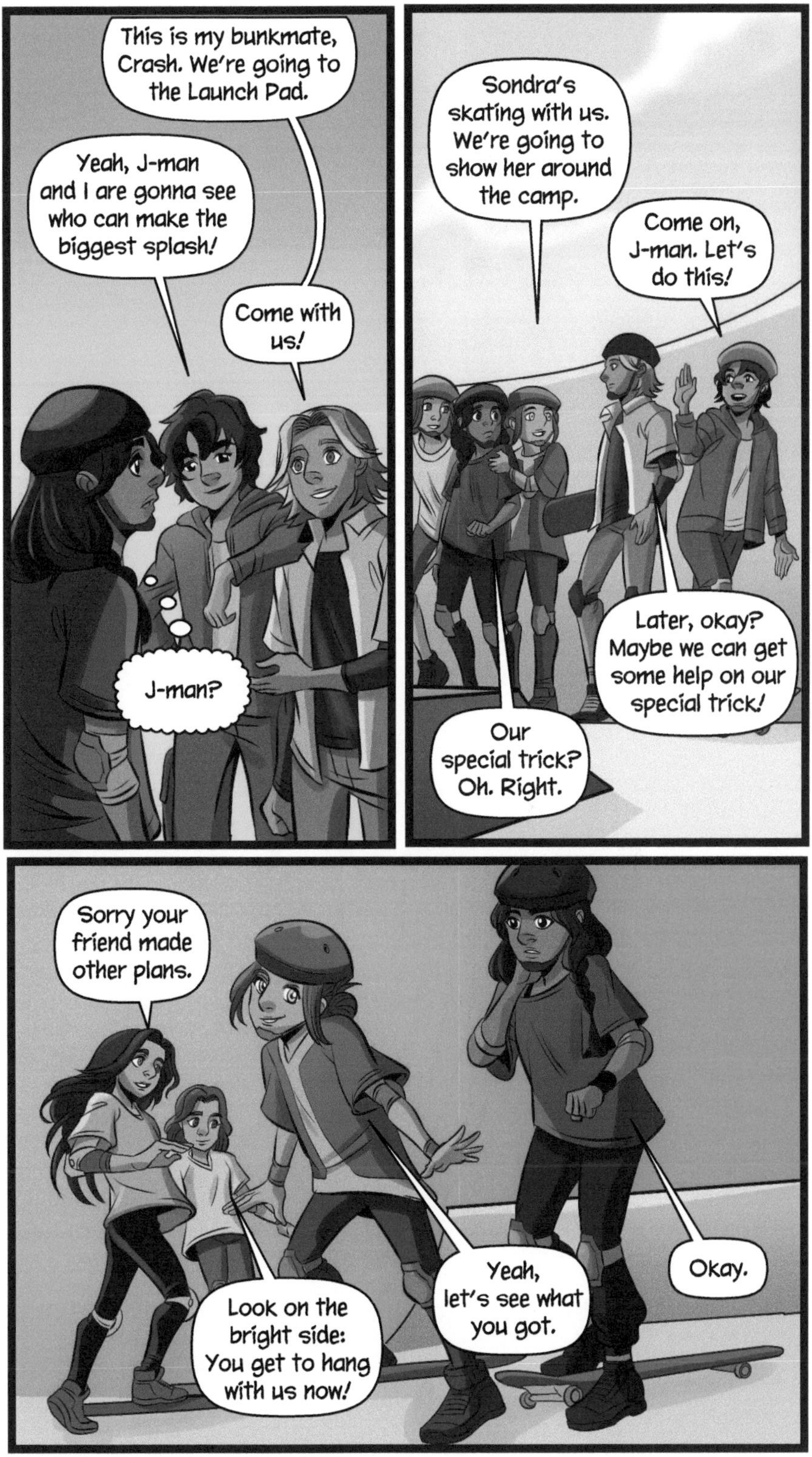
This is my bunkmate, Crash. We're going to the Launch Pad.
Yeah, J-man and I are gonna see who can make the biggest splash!
Come with us!
J-man?
Sondra's skating with us. We're going to show her around the camp.
Come on, J-man. Let's do this!
Later, okay? Maybe we can get some help on our special trick!
Our special trick? Oh. Right.
Sorry your friend made other plans.
Look on the bright side: You get to hang with us now!
Yeah, let's see what you got.
Okay.

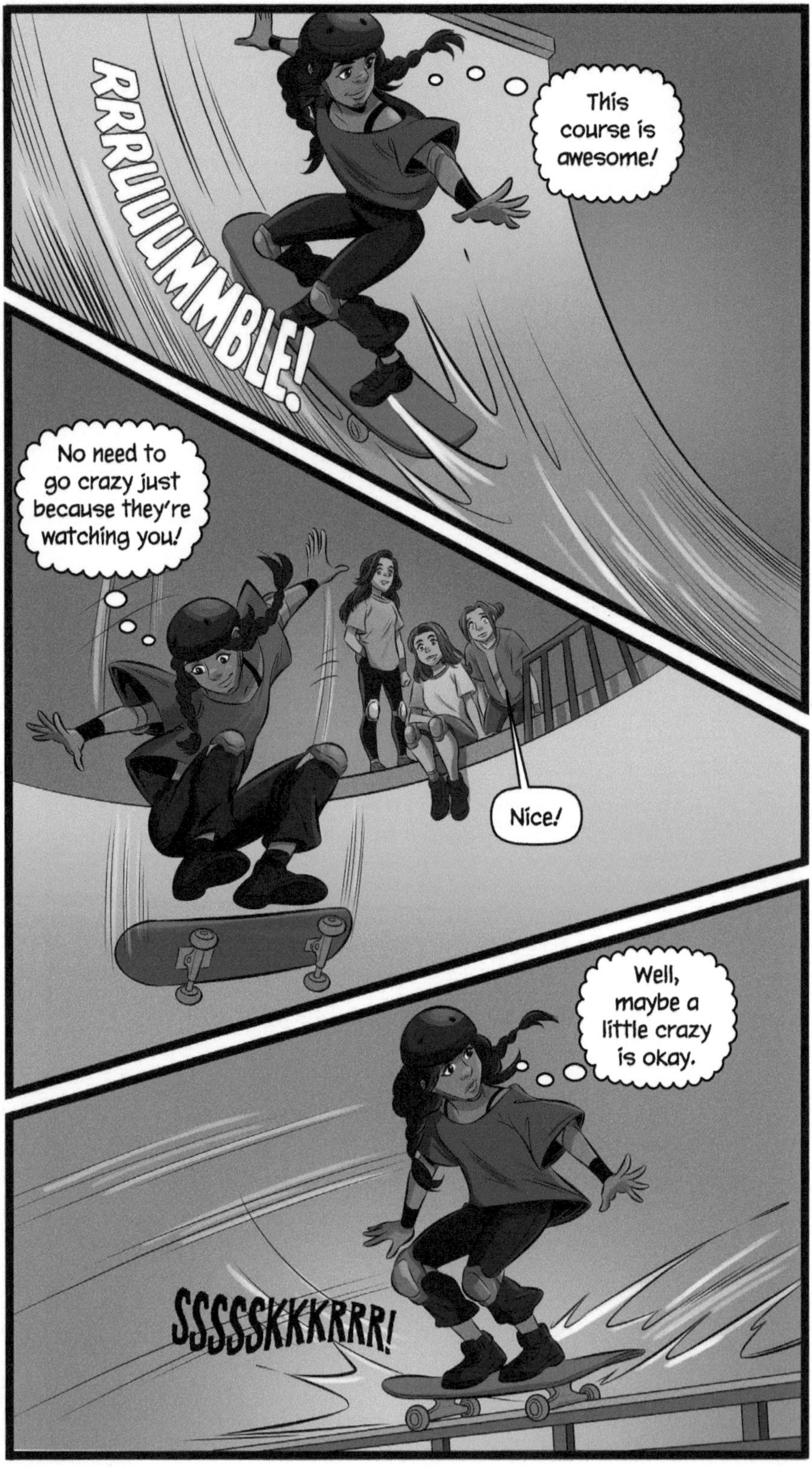

RRRUUUMMBLE!
This course is awesome!
No need to go crazy just because they're watching you!
Nice!
Well, maybe a little crazy is okay.
SSSSSKKKRRR!

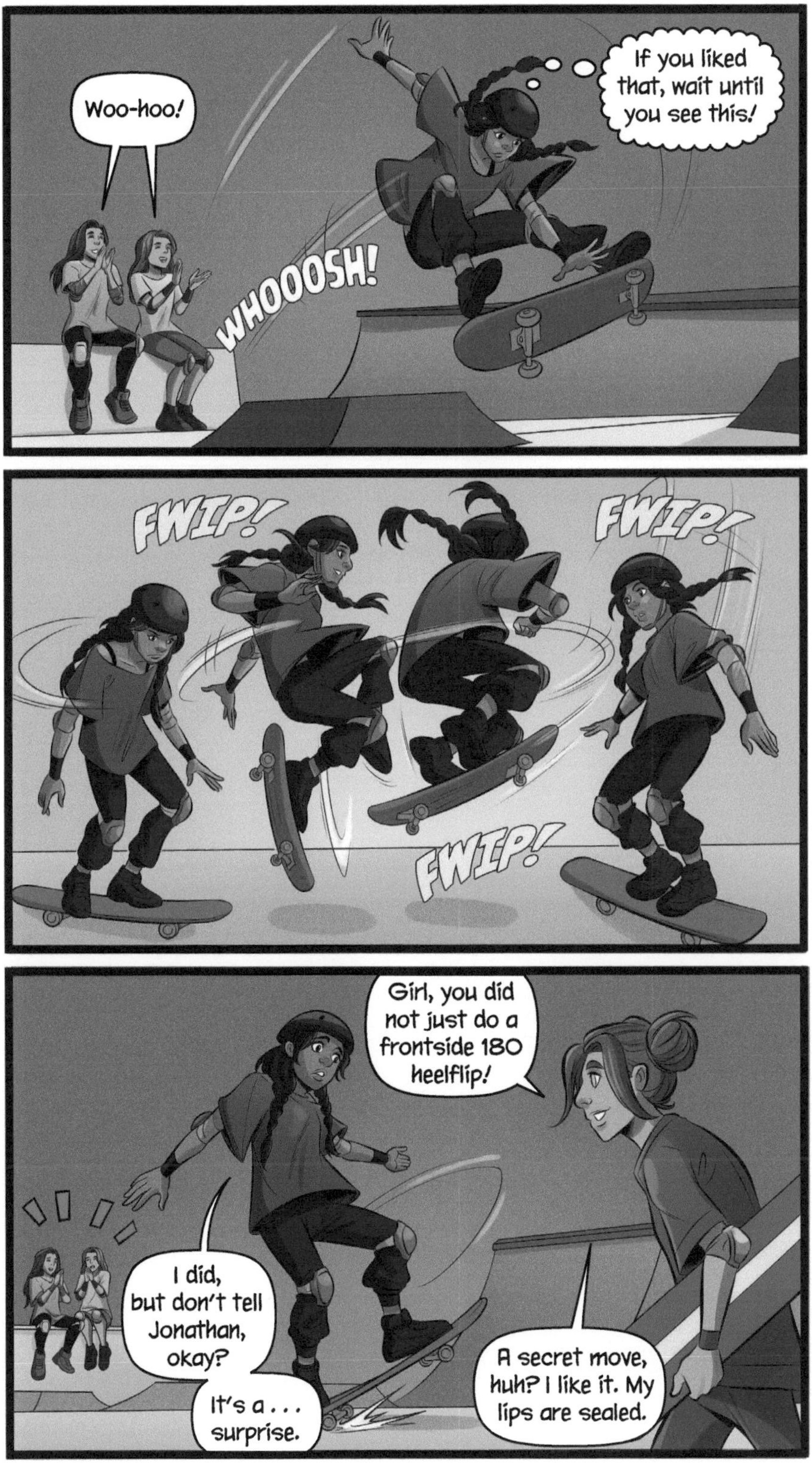
Woo-hoo!
If you liked that, wait until you see this!
WHOOOSH!
FWIP!
FWIP!
FWIP!
Girl, you did not just do a frontside 180 heelflip!
I did, but don't tell Jonathan, okay?
It's a . . . surprise.
A secret move, huh? I like it. My lips are sealed.

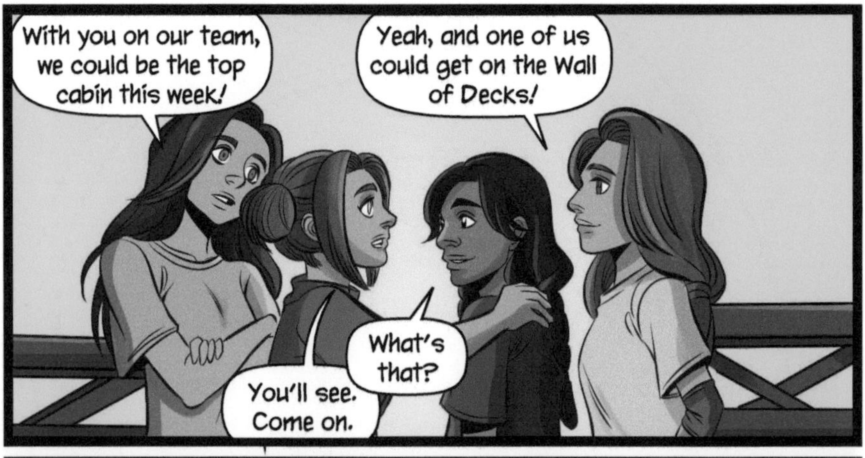
With you on our team, we could be the top cabin this week!
Yeah, and one of us could get on the Wall of Decks!
What's that?
You'll see. Come on.
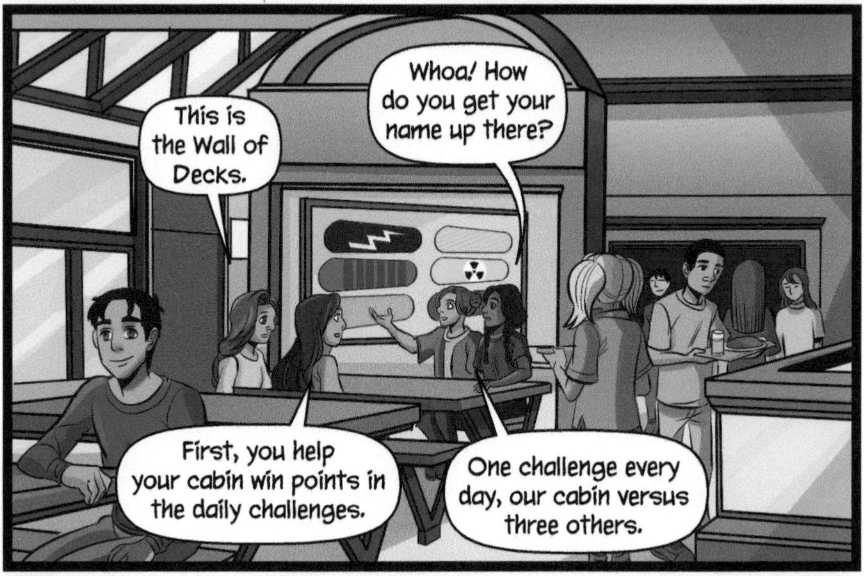
This is the Wall of Decks.
Whoa! How do you get your name up there?
First, you help your cabin win points in the daily challenges.
One challenge every day, our cabin versus three others.
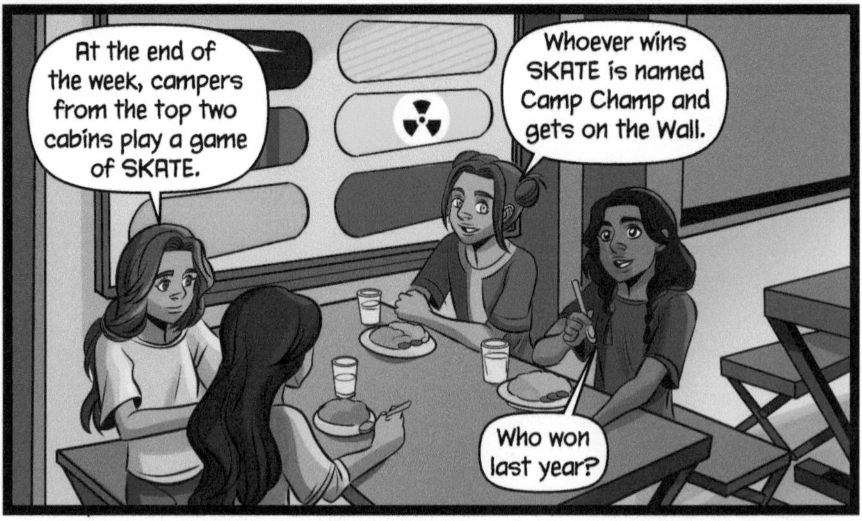
At the end of the week, campers from the top two cabins play a game of SKATE.
Whoever wins SKATE is named Camp Champ and gets on the Wall.
Who won last year?

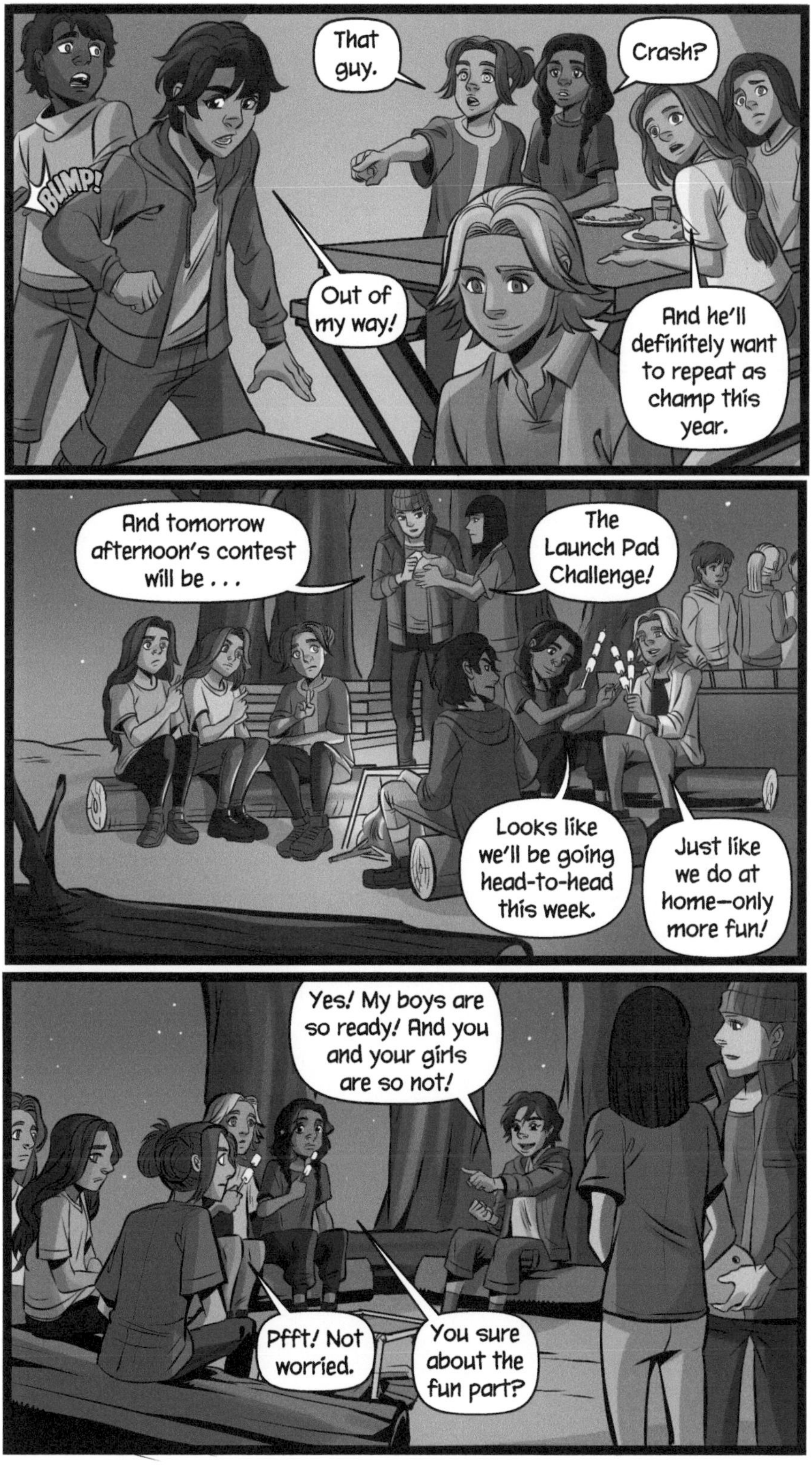
BUMP!
That guy.
Crash?
Out of my way!
And he'll definitely want to repeat as champ this year.
And tomorrow afternoon's contest will be . . .
The Launch Pad Challenge!
Looks like we'll be going head-to-head this week.
Just like we do at home—only more fun!
Yes! My boys are so ready! And you and your girls are so not!
Pfft! Not worried.
You sure about the fun part?

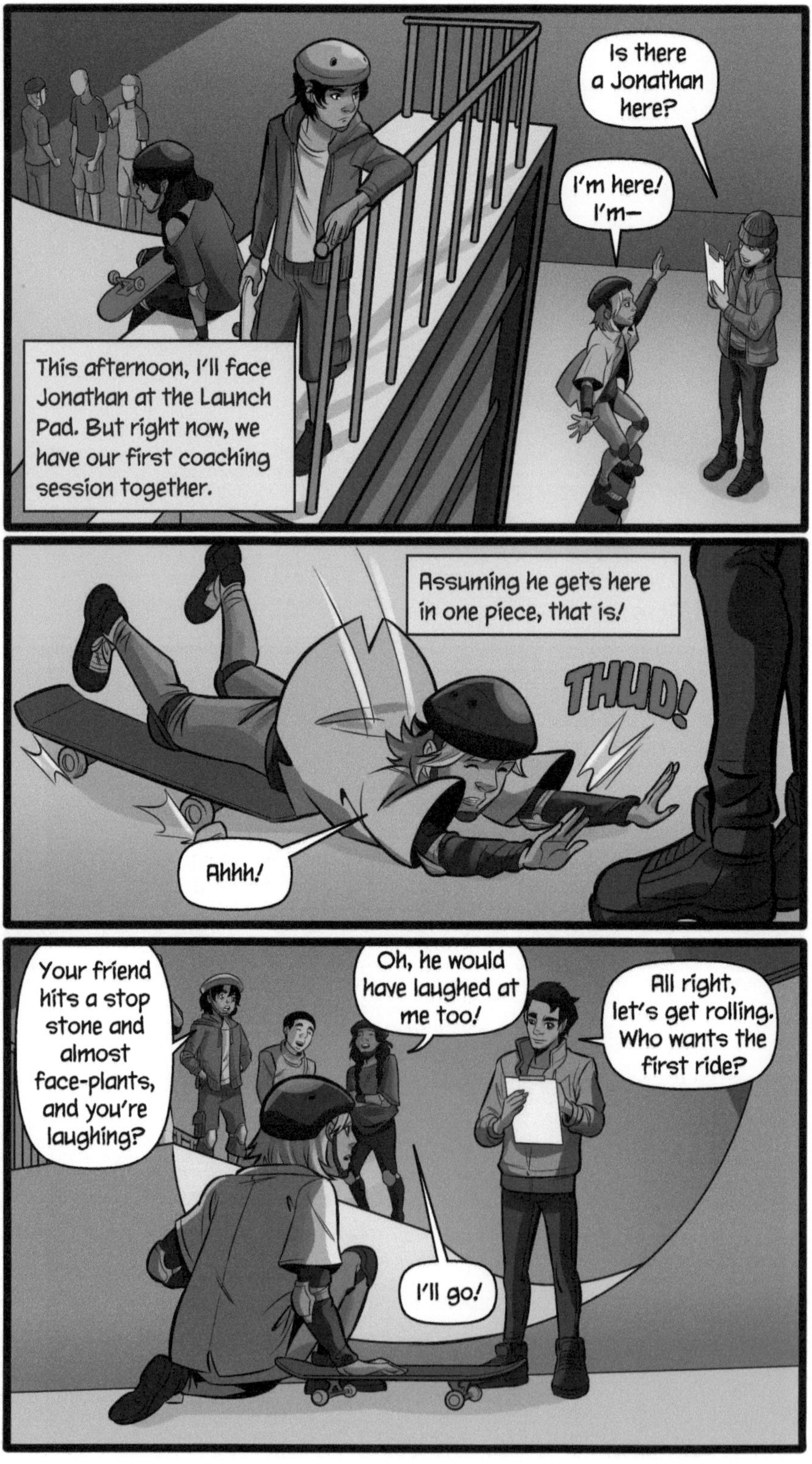
This afternoon, I'll face Jonathan at the Launch Pad. But right now, we have our first coaching session together.
Is there a Jonathan here?
I'm here! I'm—
Assuming he gets here in one piece, that is!
THUD!
Ahhh!
Your friend hits a stop stone and almost face-plants, and you're laughing?
Oh, he would have laughed at me too!
All right, let's get rolling. Who wants the first ride?
I'll go!

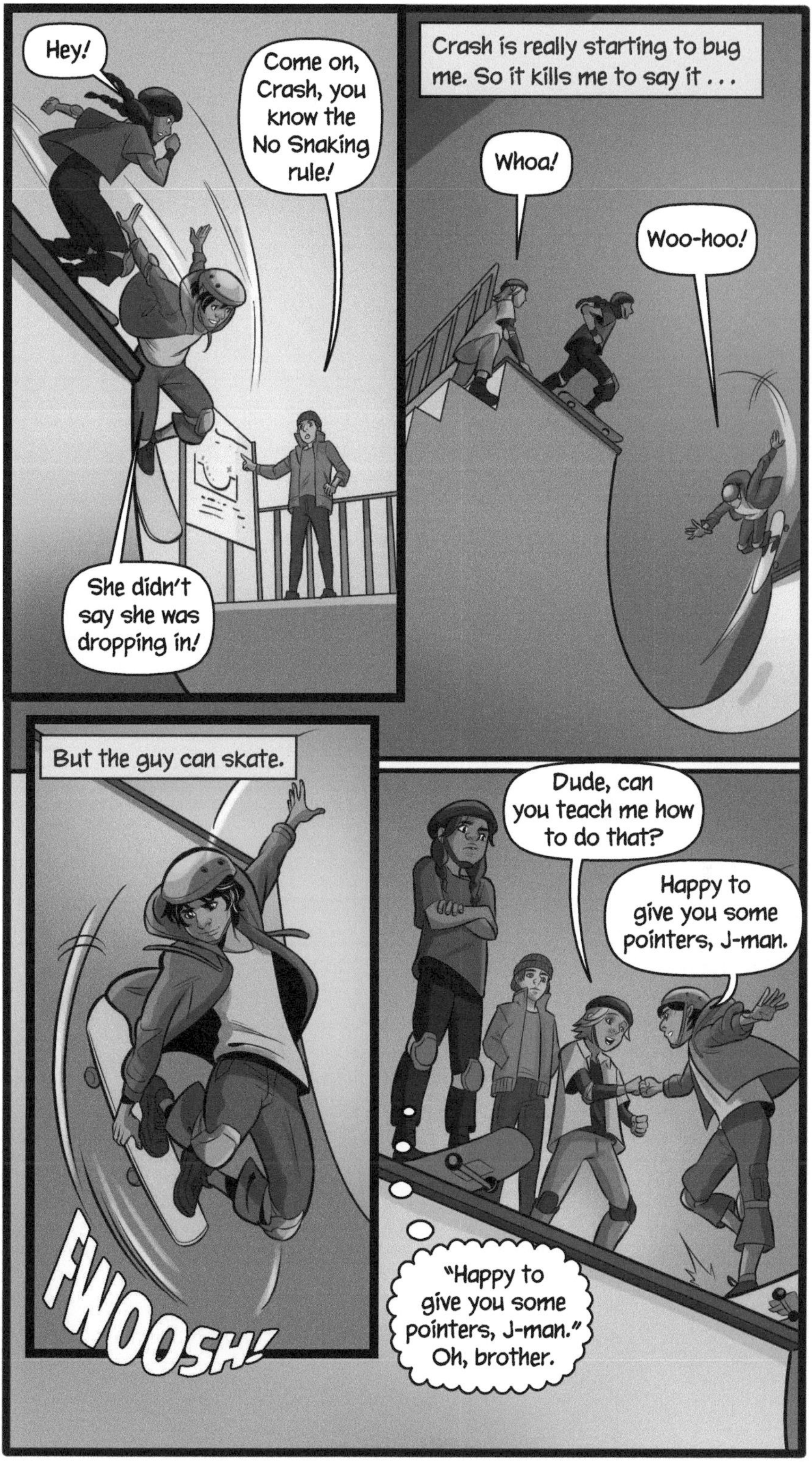
Hey!
Come on, Crash, you know the No Snaking rule!
She didn't say she was dropping in!
Crash is really starting to bug me. So it kills me to say it . . .
Whoa!
Woo-hoo!
But the guy can skate.
FWOOSH!
Dude, can you teach me how to do that?
Happy to give you some pointers, J-man.
"Happy to give you some pointers, J-man." Oh, brother.

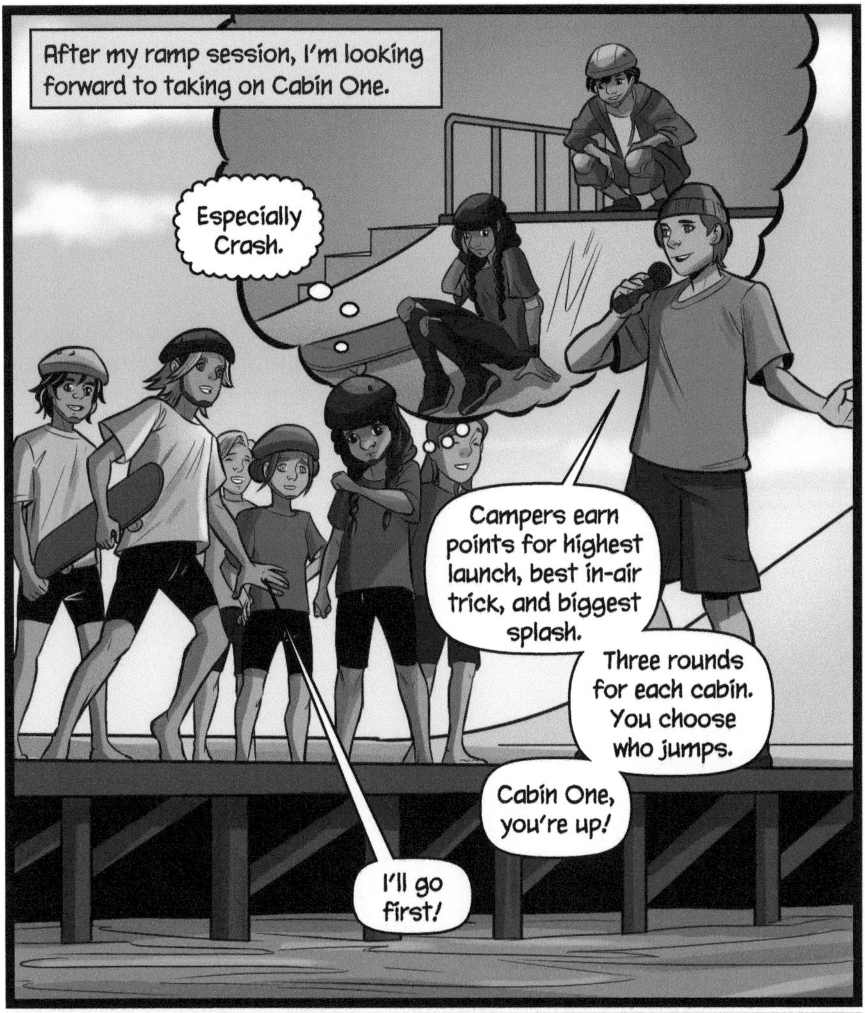
After my ramp session, I'm looking forward to taking on Cabin One.
Especially Crash.
Campers earn points for highest launch, best in-air trick, and biggest splash.
Three rounds for each cabin. You choose who jumps.
Cabin One, you're up!
I'll go first!

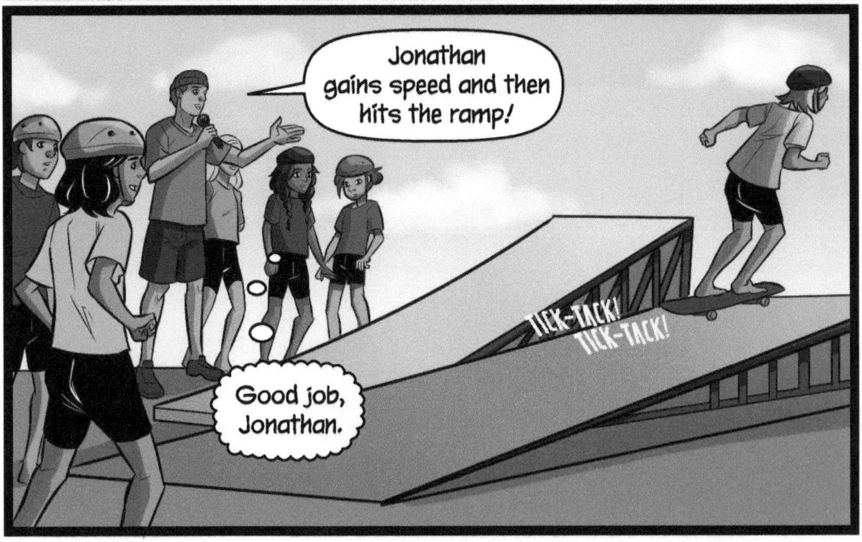
Jonathan gains speed and then hits the ramp!
TICK-TACK! TICK-TACK!
Good job, Jonathan.

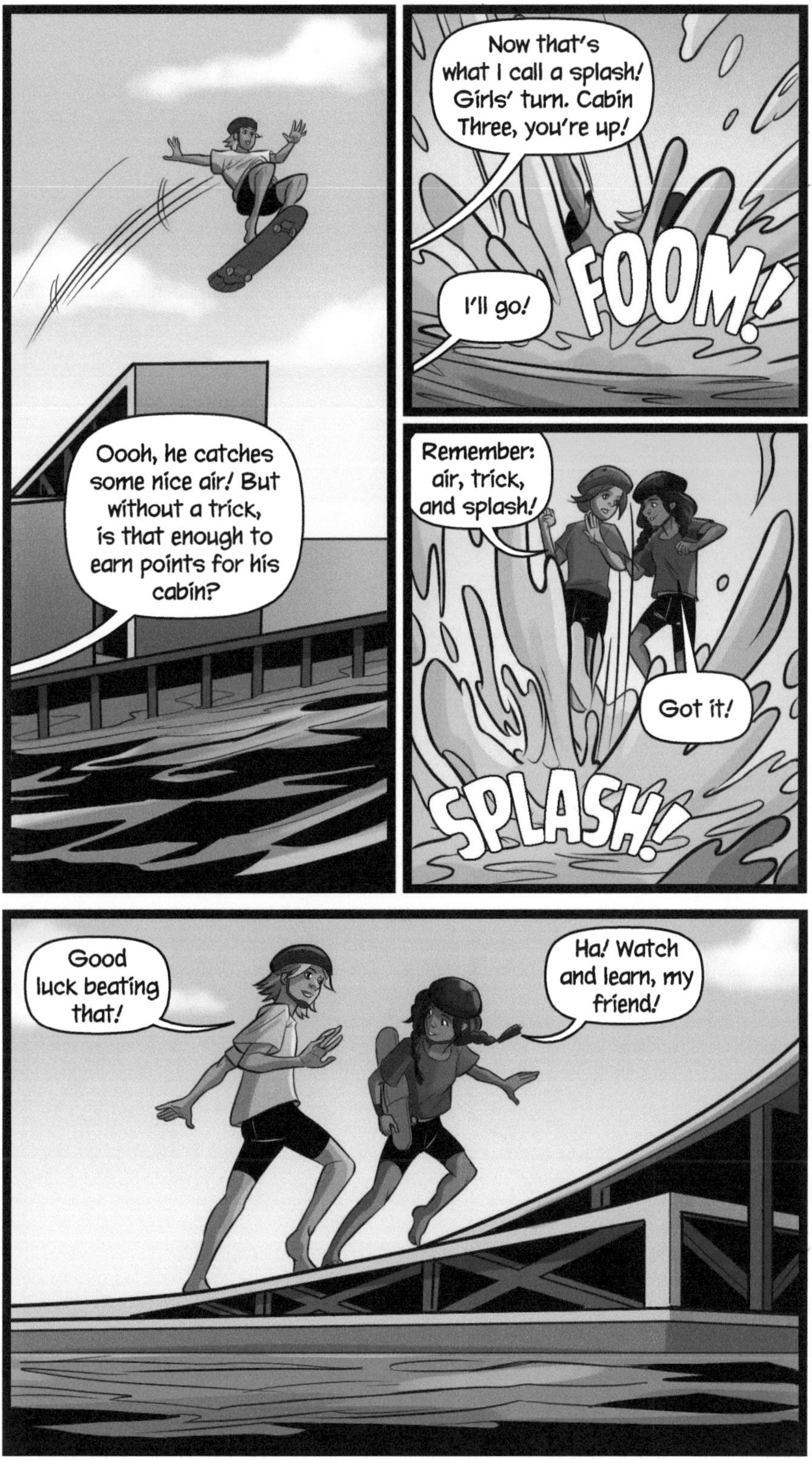

Oooh, he catches some nice air! But without a trick, is that enough to earn points for his cabin?
Now that's what I call a splash! Girls' turn. Cabin Three, you're up!
FOOM!
I'll go!
Remember: air, trick, and splash!
Got it!
SPLASH!
Good luck beating that!
Ha! Watch and learn, my friend!

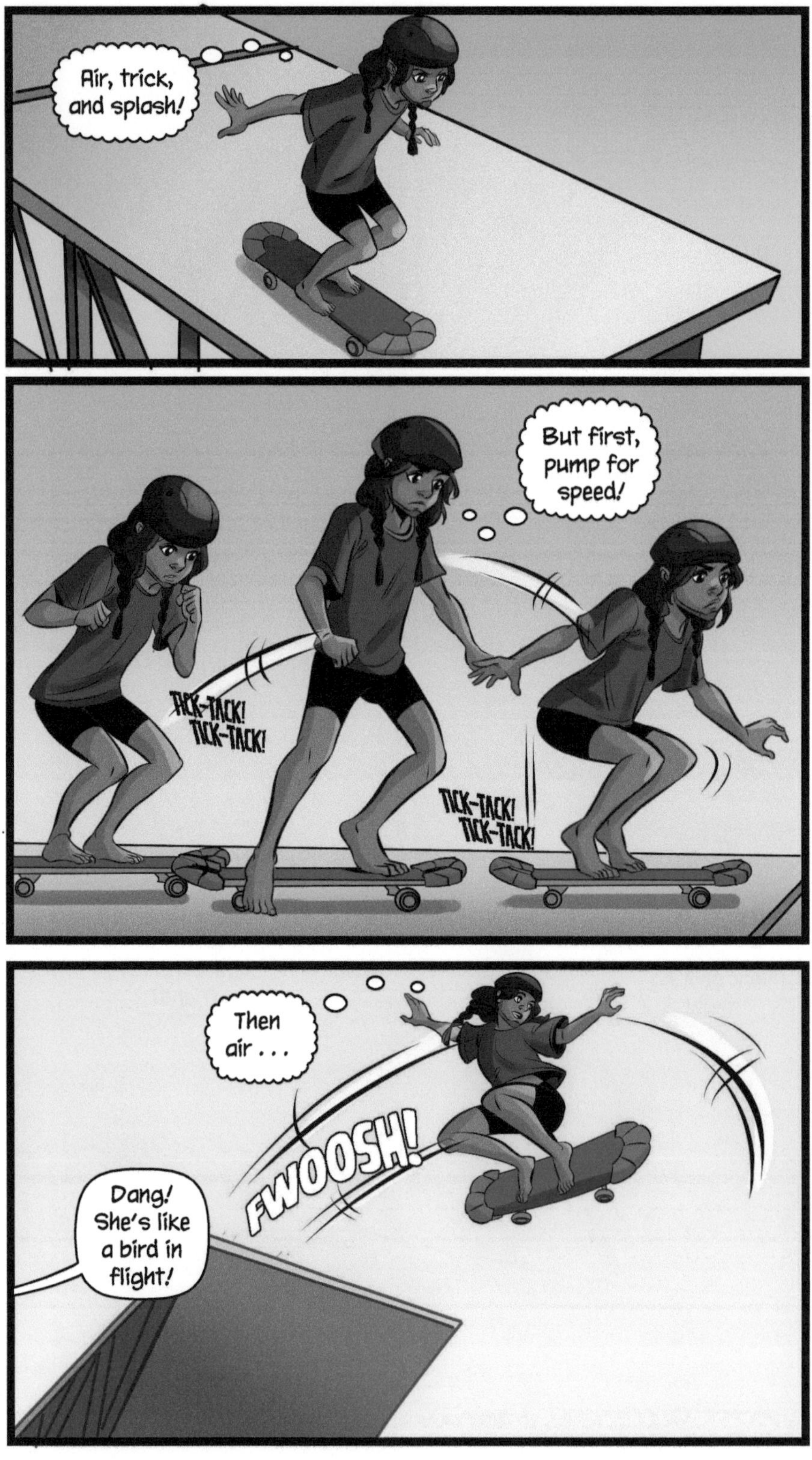

Air, trick, and splash!
But first, pump for speed!
TICK-TACK! TICK-TACK!
TICK-TACK! TICK-TACK!
Then air . . .
FWOOSH!
Dang! She's like a bird in flight!

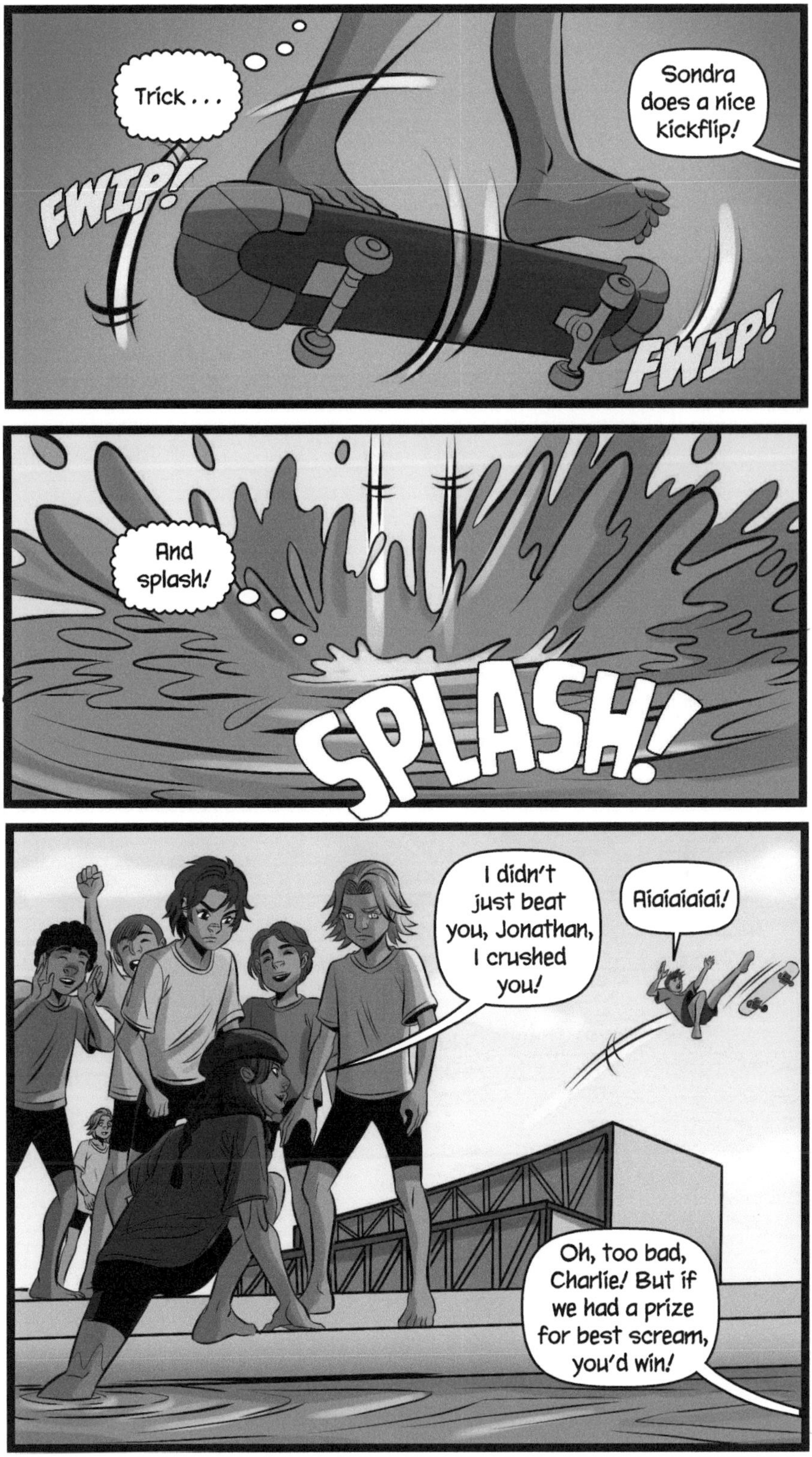

Trick . . .
Sondra does a nice kickflip!
FWIP!
FWIP!
And splash!
SPLASH!
I didn't just beat you, Jonathan, I crushed you!
Aiaiaiaiai!
Oh, too bad, Charlie! But if we had a prize for best scream, you'd win!

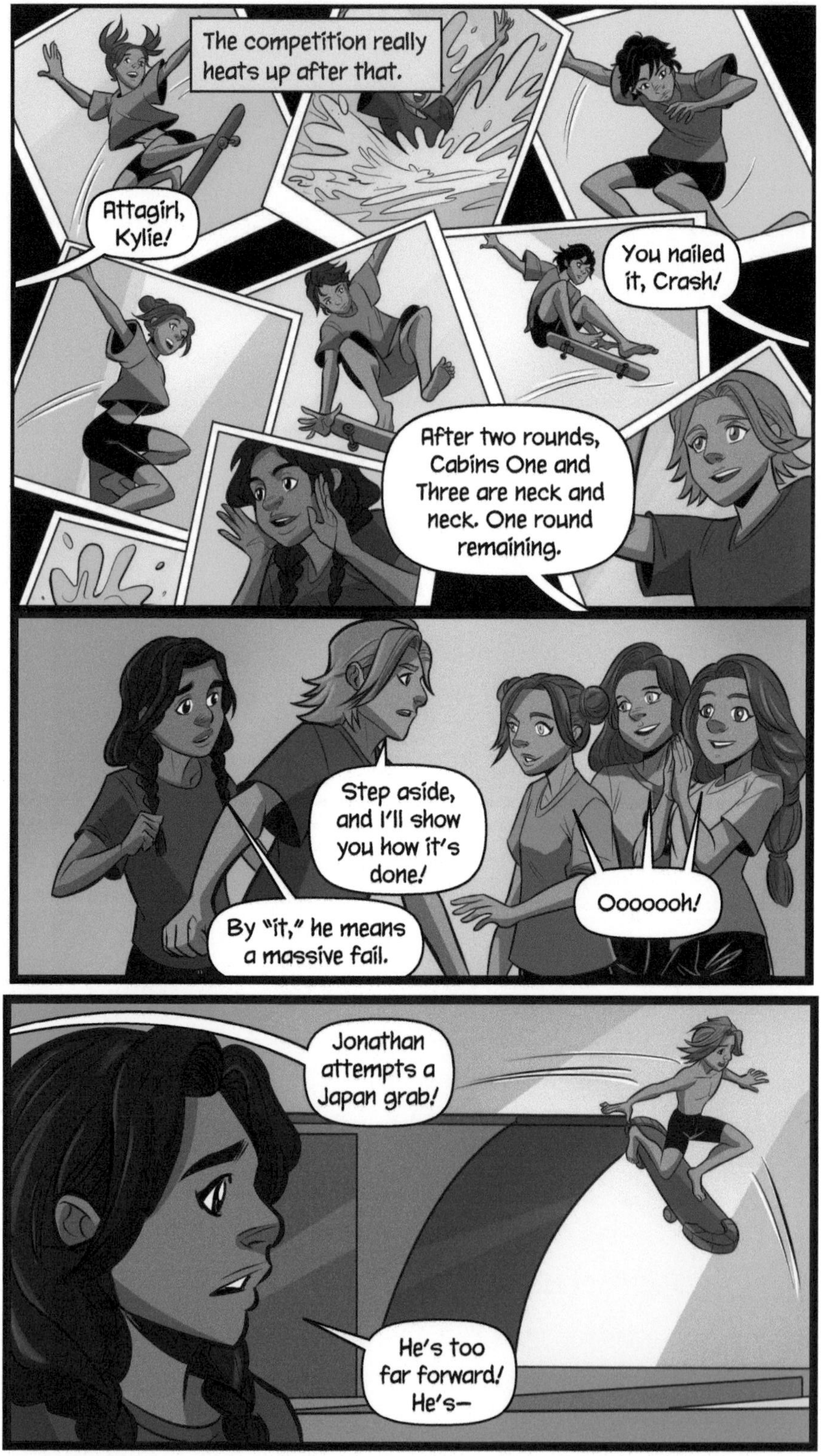
The competition really heats up after that.
Attagirl, Kylie!
You nailed it, Crash!
After two rounds, Cabins One and Three are neck and neck. One round remaining.
Step aside, and I'll show you how it's done!
By "it," he means a massive fail.
Oooooh!
Jonathan attempts a Japan grab!
He's too far forward! He's—

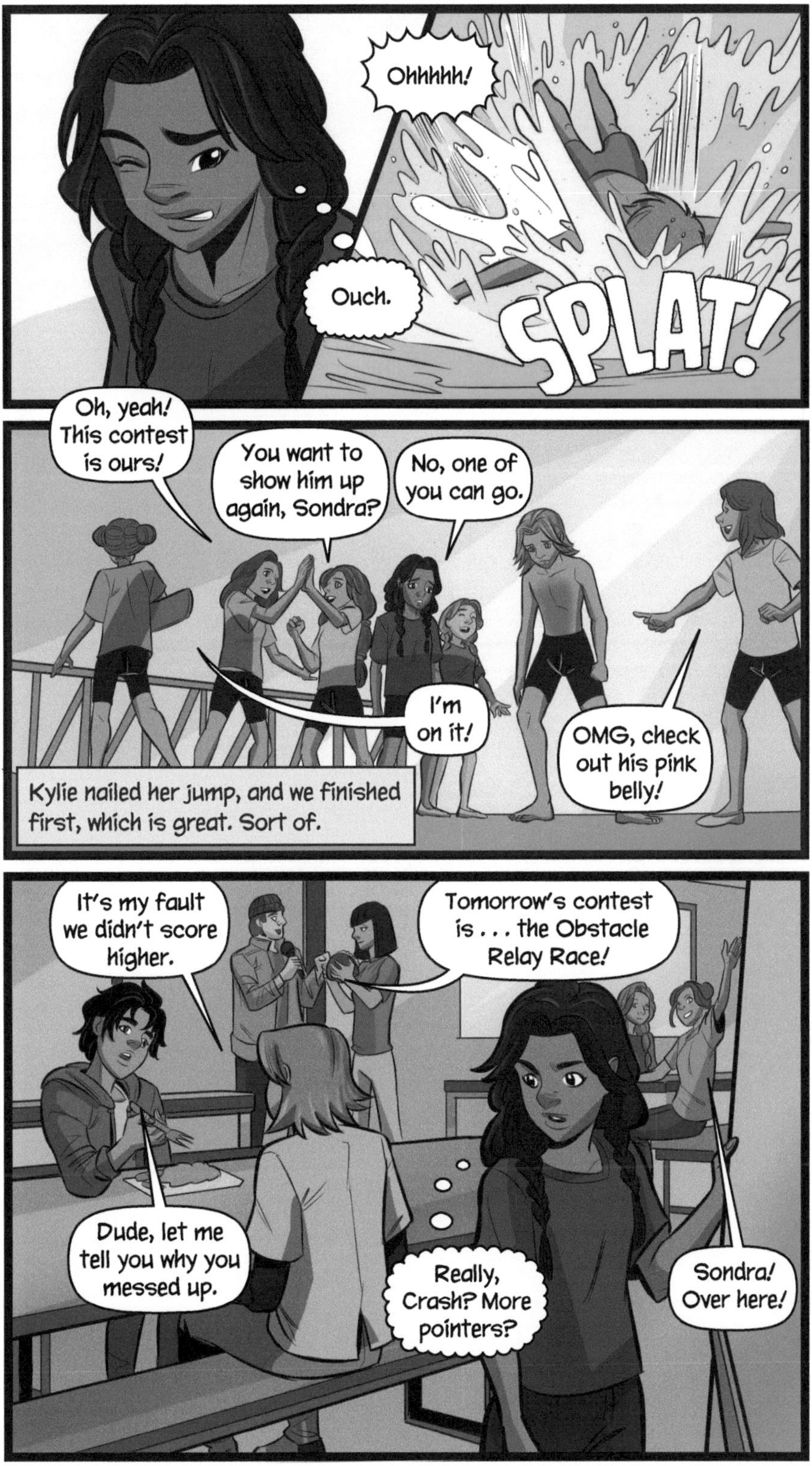
Ohhhhh!
Ouch.
SPLAT!
Oh, yeah! This contest is ours!
You want to show him up again, Sondra?
No, one of you can go.
I'm on it!
OMG, check out his pink belly!
Kylie nailed her jump, and we finished first, which is great. Sort of.
It's my fault we didn't score higher.
Tomorrow's contest is . . . the Obstacle Relay Race!
Dude, let me tell you why you messed up.
Really, Crash? More pointers?
Sondra! Over here!

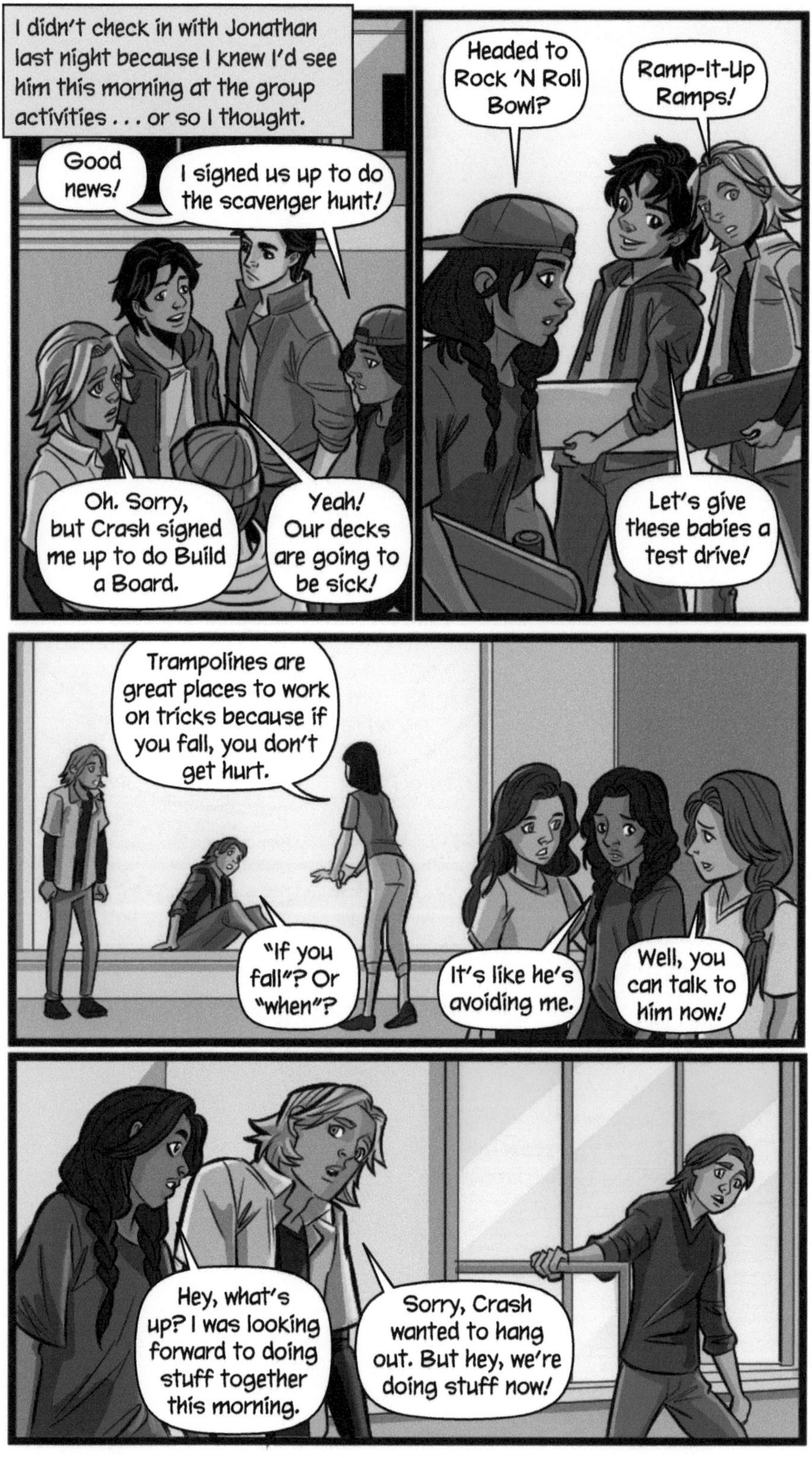
I didn't check in with Jonathan last night because I knew I'd see him this morning at the group activities . . . or so I thought.
Good news!
I signed us up to do the scavenger hunt!
Oh. Sorry, but Crash signed me up to do Build a Board.
Yeah! Our decks are going to be sick!
Headed to Rock 'N Roll Bowl?
Ramp-It-Up Ramps!
Let's give these babies a test drive!
Trampolines are great places to work on tricks because if you fall, you don't get hurt.
"If you fall"? Or "when"?
It's like he's avoiding me.
Well, you can talk to him now!
Hey, what's up? I was looking forward to doing stuff together this morning.
Sorry, Crash wanted to hang out. But hey, we're doing stuff now!

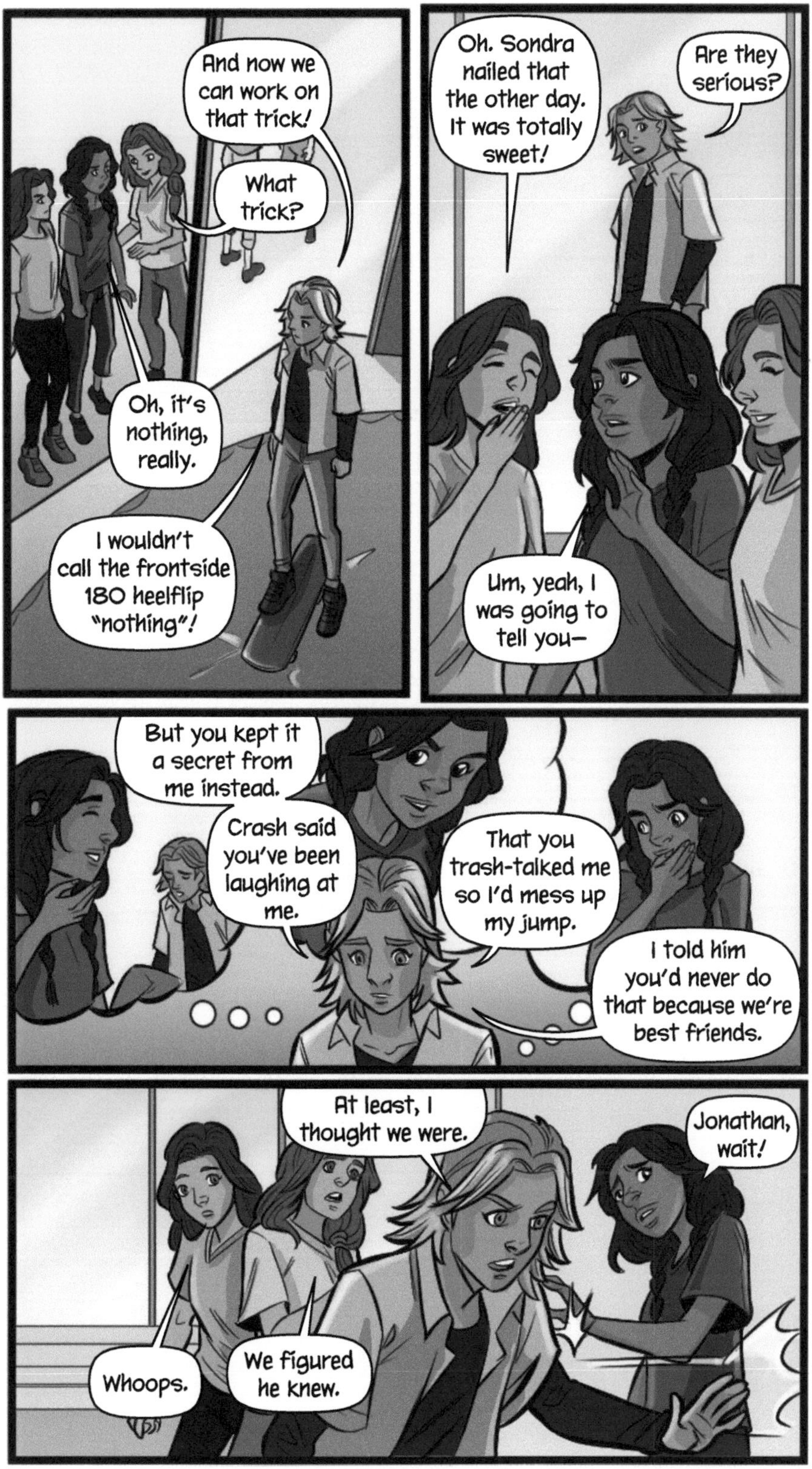
And now we can work on that trick!
What trick?
Oh, it's nothing, really.
I wouldn't call the frontside 180 heelflip "nothing"!
Oh. Sondra nailed that the other day. It was totally sweet!
Are they serious?
Um, yeah, I was going to tell you—
But you kept it a secret from me instead.
Crash said you've been laughing at me.
That you trash-talked me so I'd mess up my jump.
I told him you'd never do that because we're best friends.
At least, I thought we were.
Jonathan, wait!
Whoops.
We figured he knew.

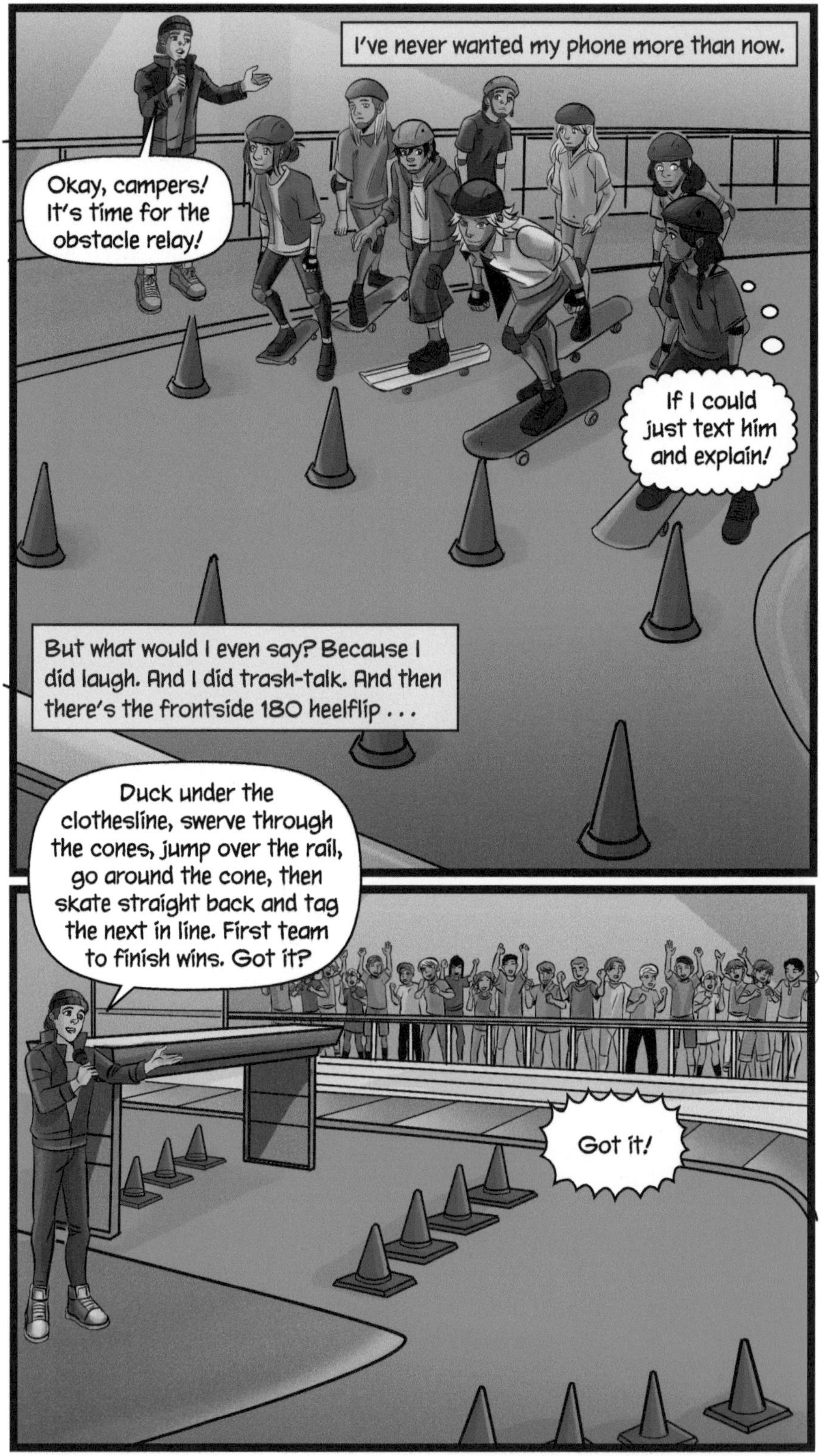
I've never wanted my phone more than now.
Okay, campers! It's time for the obstacle relay!
If I could just text him and explain!
But what would I even say? Because I did laugh. And I did trash-talk. And then there's the frontside 180 heelflip . . .
Duck under the clothesline, swerve through the cones, jump over the rail, go around the cone, then skate straight back and tag the next in line. First team to finish wins. Got it?
Got it!

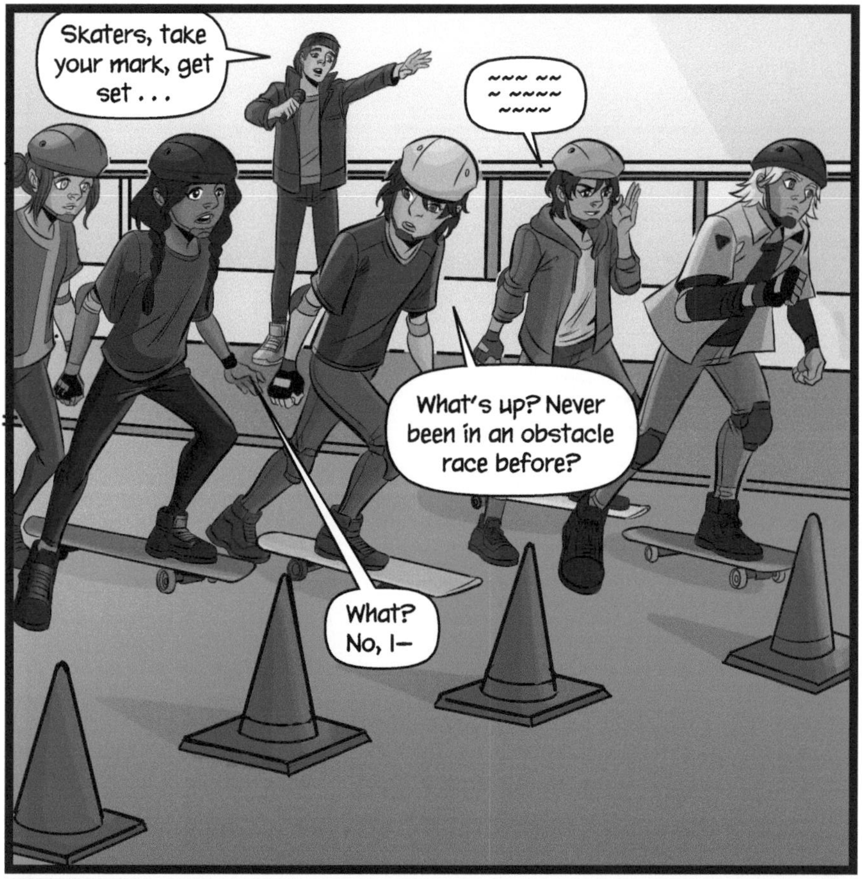
Skaters, take your mark, get set . . .
~~~ ~~ ~ ~~~~ ~~~~
What's up? Never been in an obstacle race before?
What? No, I—

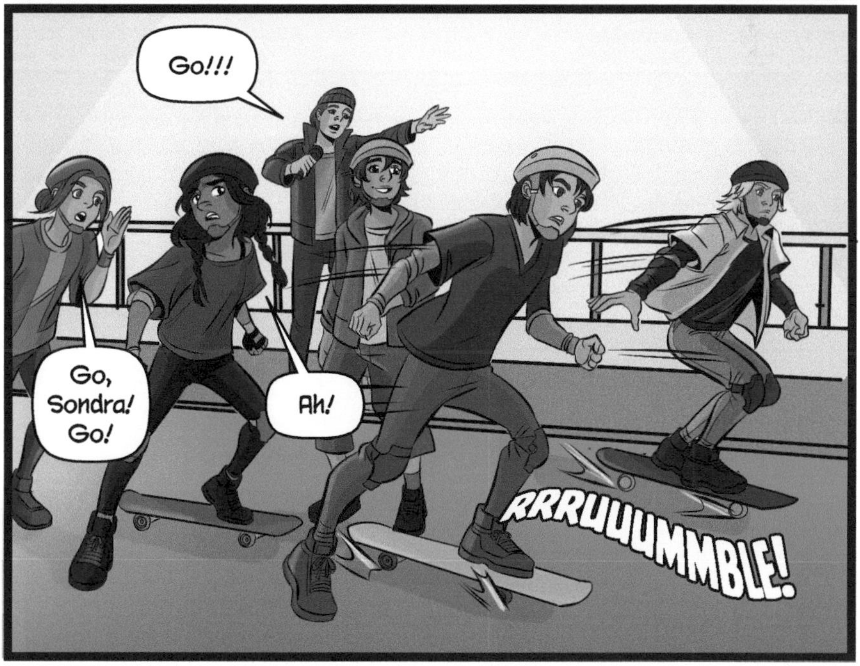
Go!!!
Go, Sondra! Go!
Ah!
RRRUUUMMBLE!
~~~

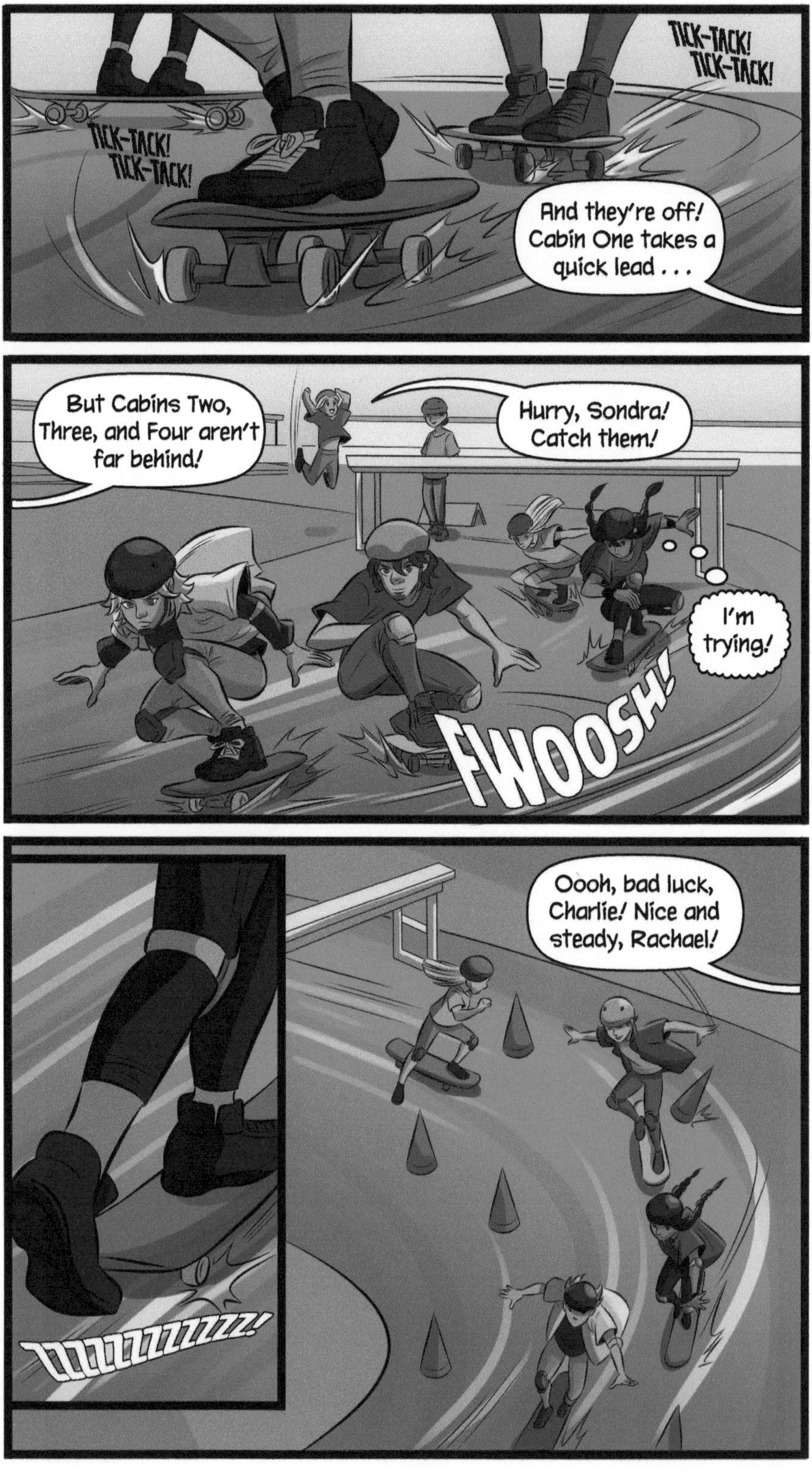

TICK-TACK!
TICK-TACK!
TICK-TACK!
TICK-TACK!
And they're off! Cabin One takes a quick lead . . .
But Cabins Two, Three, and Four aren't far behind!
Hurry, Sondra! Catch them!
I'm trying!
FWOOSH!
Oooh, bad luck, Charlie! Nice and steady, Rachael!
ZZZZZZZZZZZZ!

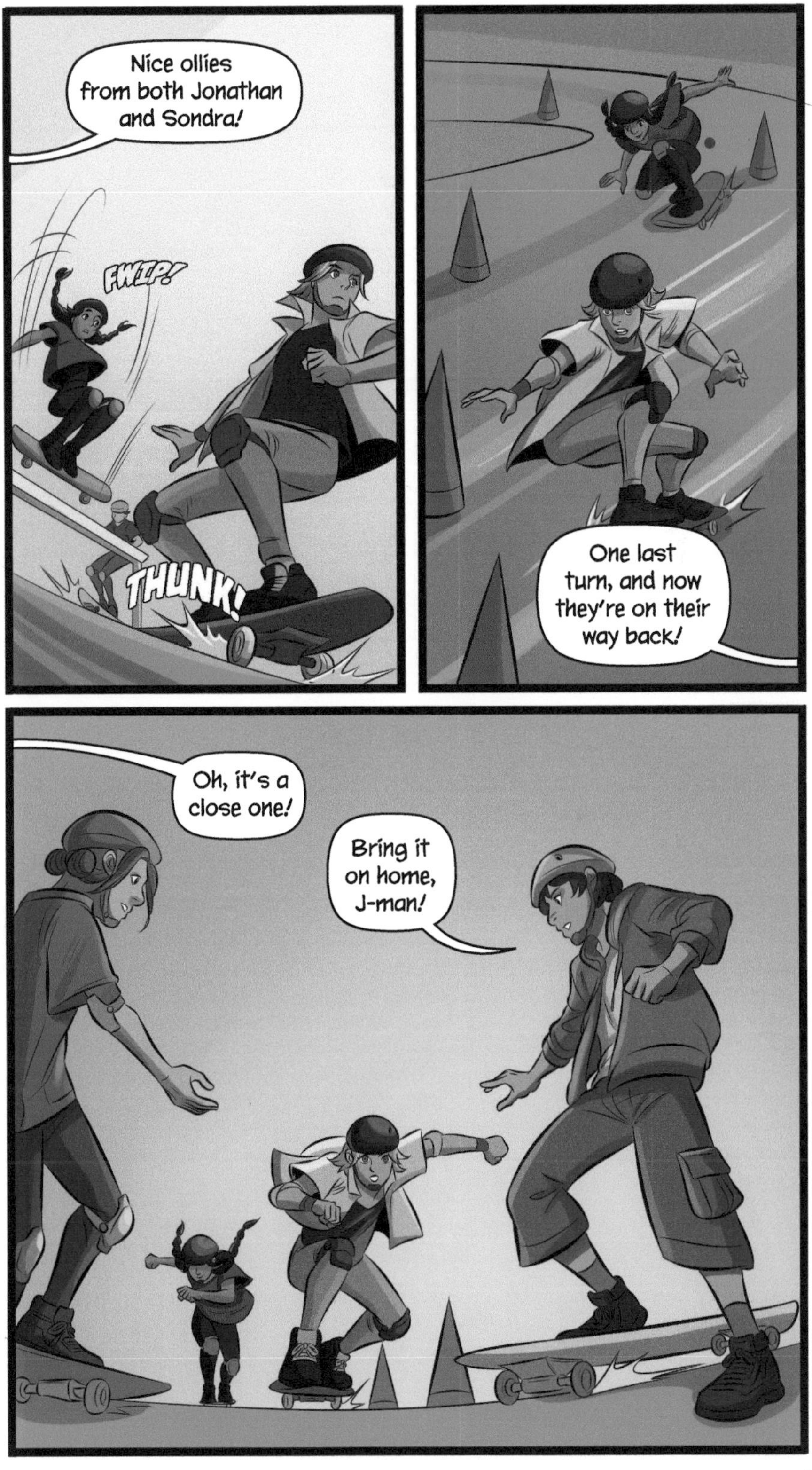

Nice ollies from both Jonathan and Sondra!
FWIP!
THUNK!
One last turn, and now they're on their way back!
Oh, it's a close one!
Bring it on home, J-man!

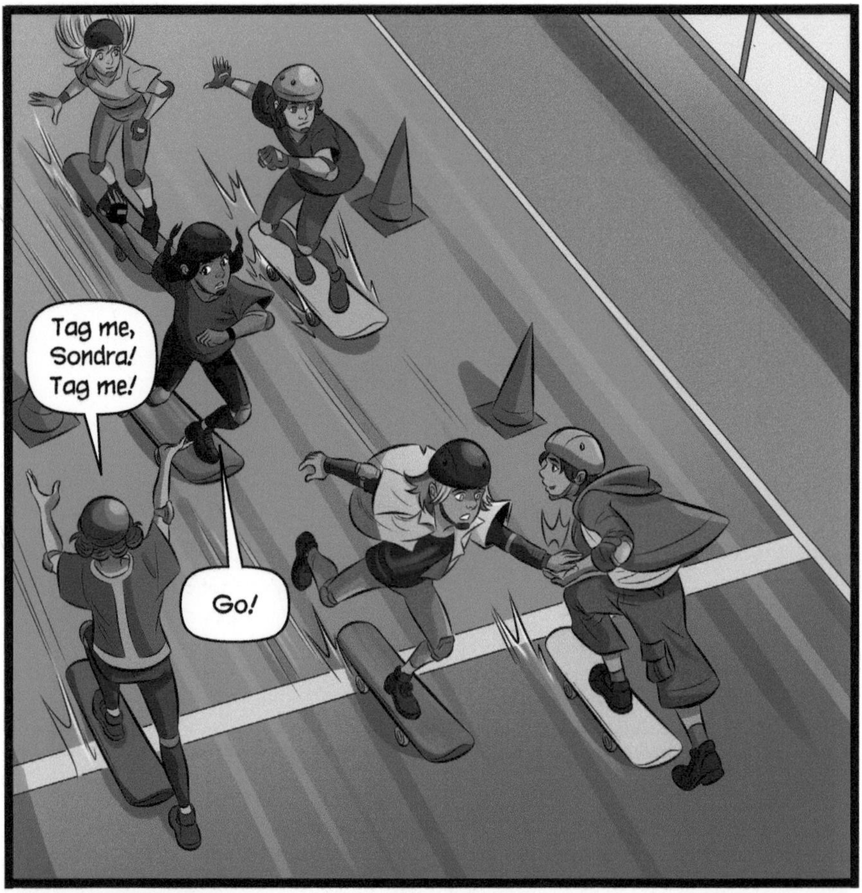

Tag me, Sondra! Tag me!
Go!

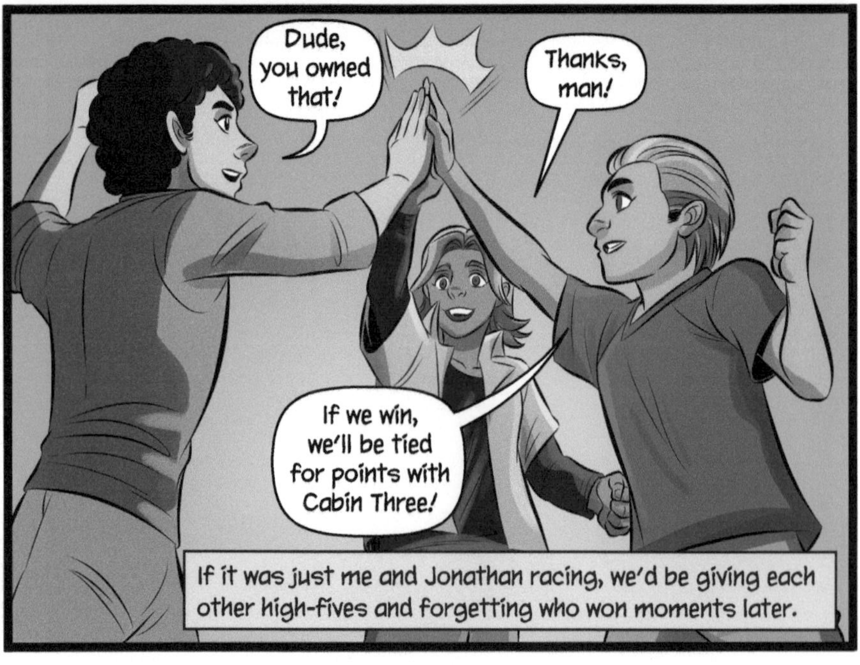

Dude, you owned that!
Thanks, man!
If we win, we'll be tied for points with Cabin Three!
If it was just me and Jonathan racing, we'd be giving each other high-fives and forgetting who won moments later.

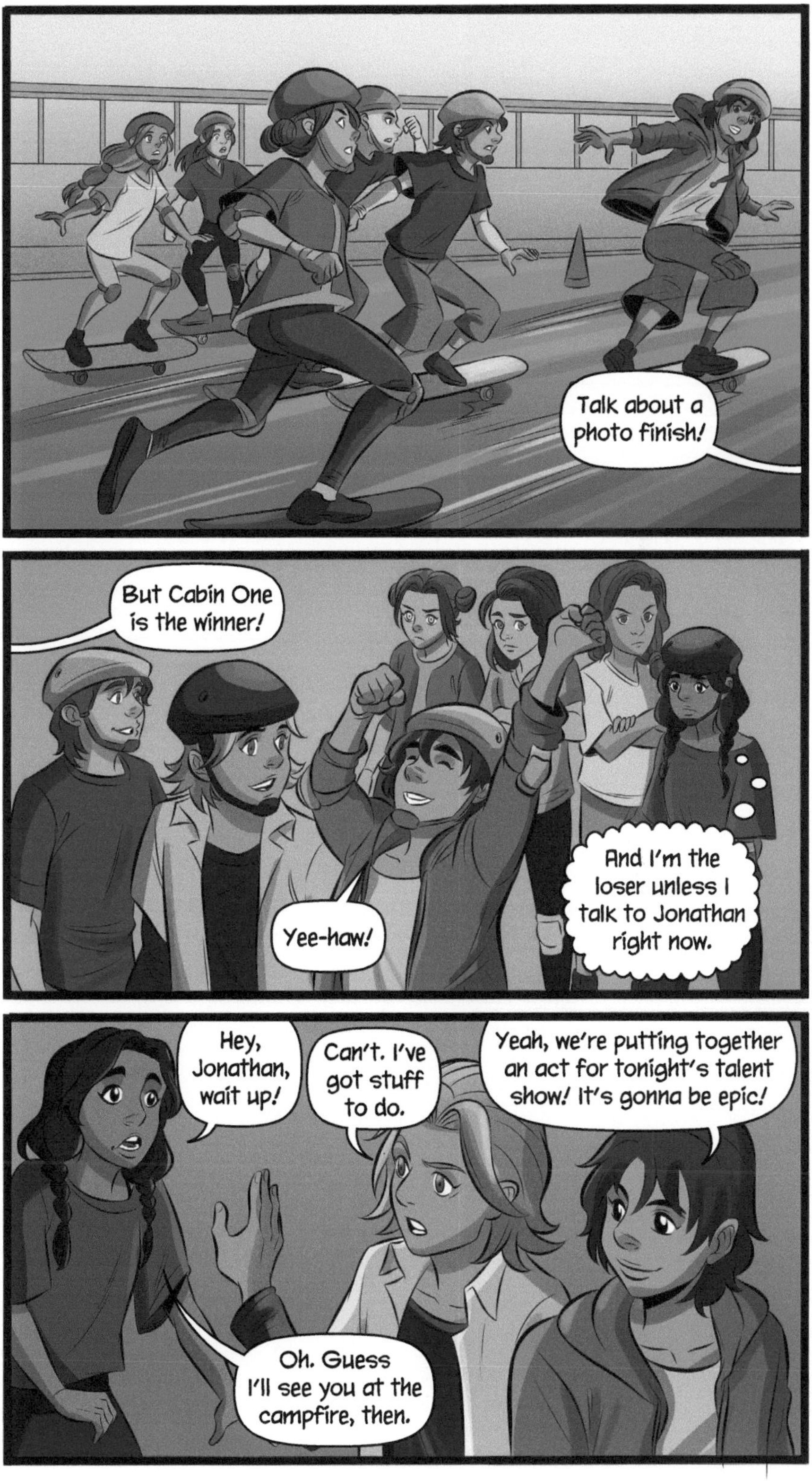
Talk about a photo finish!
But Cabin One is the winner!
Yee-haw!
And I'm the loser unless I talk to Jonathan right now.
Hey, Jonathan, wait up!
Can't. I've got stuff to do.
Yeah, we're putting together an act for tonight's talent show! It's gonna be epic!
Oh. Guess I'll see you at the campfire, then.

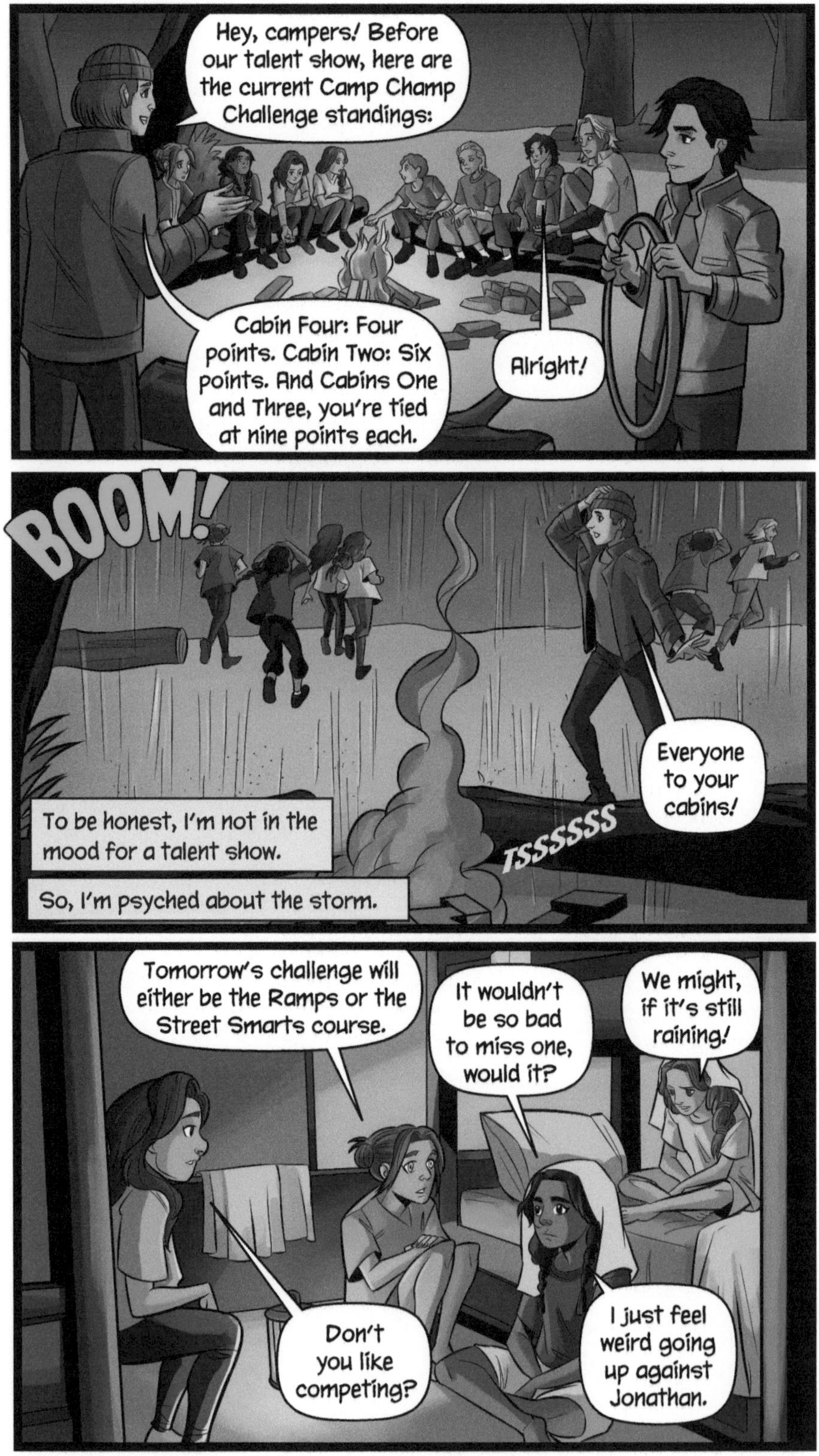

Hey, campers! Before our talent show, here are the current Camp Champ Challenge standings:
Cabin Four: Four points. Cabin Two: Six points. And Cabins One and Three, you're tied at nine points each.
Alright!
BOOM!
Everyone to your cabins!
TSSSSSS
To be honest, I'm not in the mood for a talent show.
So, I'm psyched about the storm.
Tomorrow's challenge will either be the Ramps or the Street Smarts course.
It wouldn't be so bad to miss one, would it?
We might, if it's still raining!
Don't you like competing?
I just feel weird going up against Jonathan.

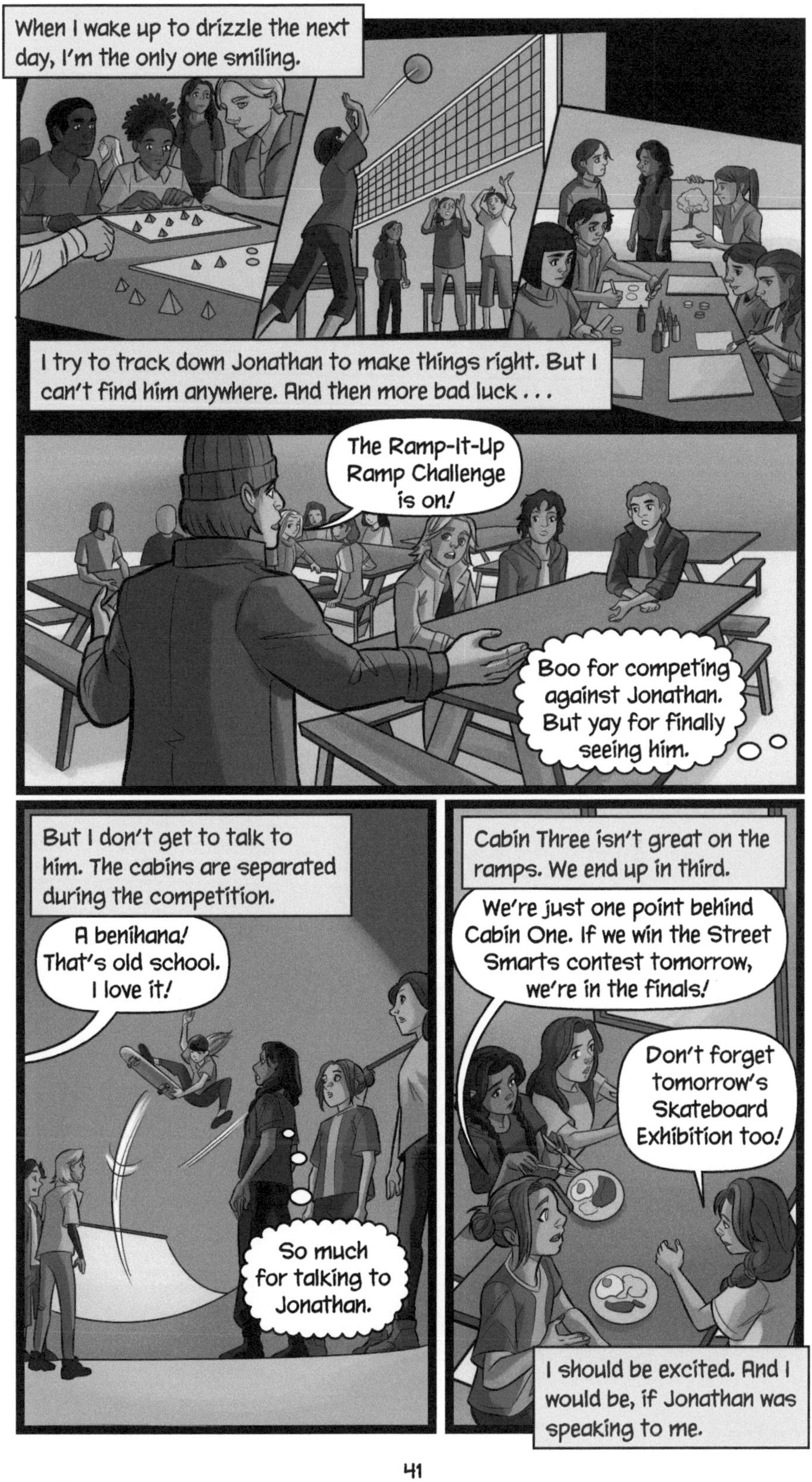

When I wake up to drizzle the next day, I'm the only one smiling.
I try to track down Jonathan to make things right. But I can't find him anywhere. And then more bad luck . . .
The Ramp-It-Up Ramp Challenge is on!
Boo for competing against Jonathan. But yay for finally seeing him.
But I don't get to talk to him. The cabins are separated during the competition.
A benihana! That's old school. I love it!
So much for talking to Jonathan.
Cabin Three isn't great on the ramps. We end up in third.
We're just one point behind Cabin One. If we win the Street Smarts contest tomorrow, we're in the finals!
Don't forget tomorrow's Skateboard Exhibition too!
I should be excited. And I would be, if Jonathan was speaking to me.

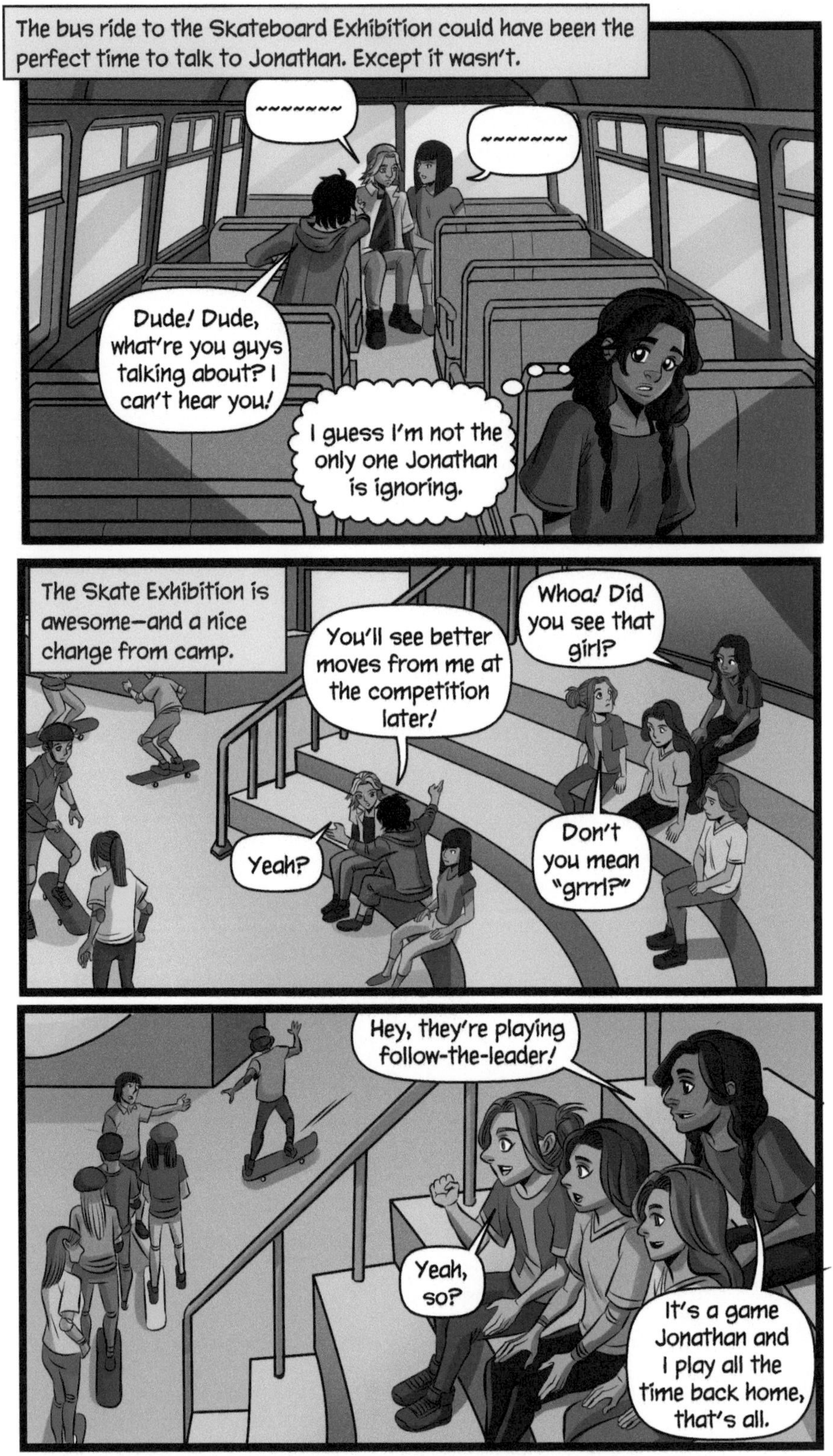
The bus ride to the Skateboard Exhibition could have been the perfect time to talk to Jonathan. Except it wasn't.
~~~~~~~
~~~~~~~
Dude! Dude, what're you guys talking about? I can't hear you!
I guess I'm not the only one Jonathan is ignoring.
The Skate Exhibition is awesome—and a nice change from camp.
You'll see better moves from me at the competition later!
Yeah?
Whoa! Did you see that girl?
Don't you mean "grrrl?"
Hey, they're playing follow-the-leader!
Yeah, so?
It's a game Jonathan and I play all the time back home, that's all.

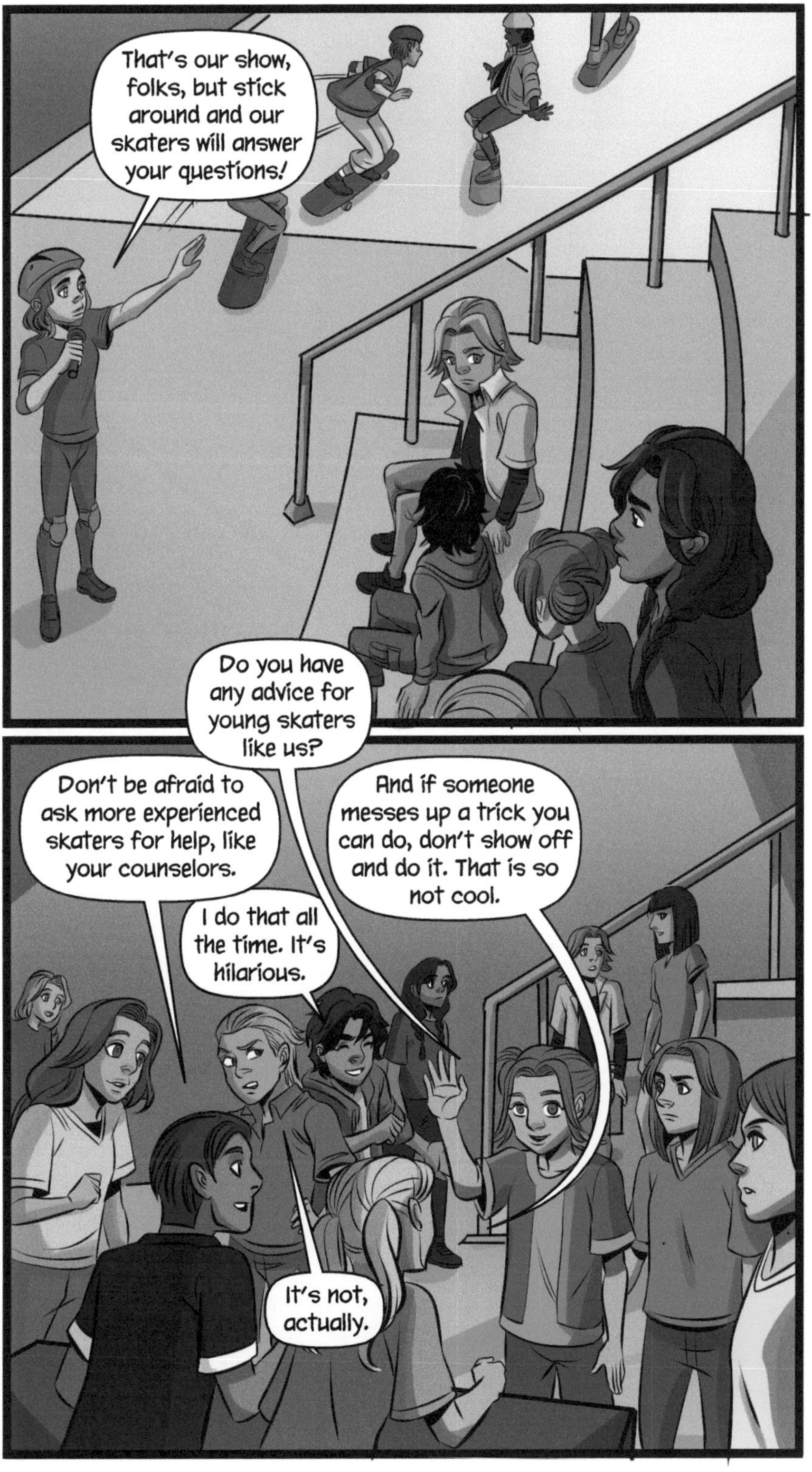
That's our show, folks, but stick around and our skaters will answer your questions!
Do you have any advice for young skaters like us?
Don't be afraid to ask more experienced skaters for help, like your counselors.
And if someone messes up a trick you can do, don't show off and do it. That is so not cool.
I do that all the time. It's hilarious.
It's not, actually.

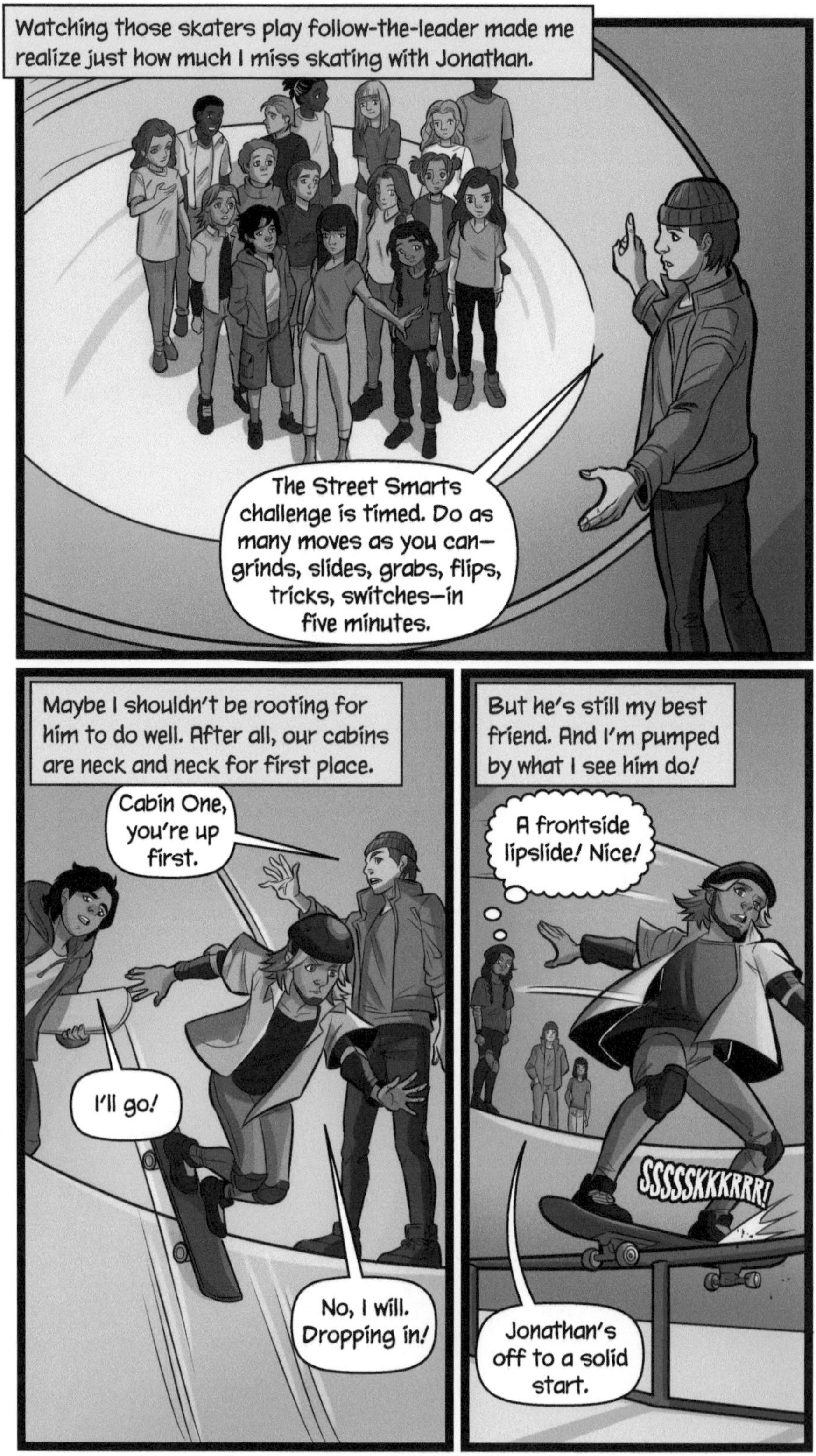

Watching those skaters play follow-the-leader made me realize just how much I miss skating with Jonathan.
The Street Smarts challenge is timed. Do as many moves as you can—grinds, slides, grabs, flips, tricks, switches—in five minutes.
Maybe I shouldn't be rooting for him to do well. After all, our cabins are neck and neck for first place.
Cabin One, you're up first.
I'll go!
No, I will. Dropping in!
But he's still my best friend. And I'm pumped by what I see him do!
A frontside lipslide! Nice!
SSSSSKKKRRR!
Jonathan's off to a solid start.

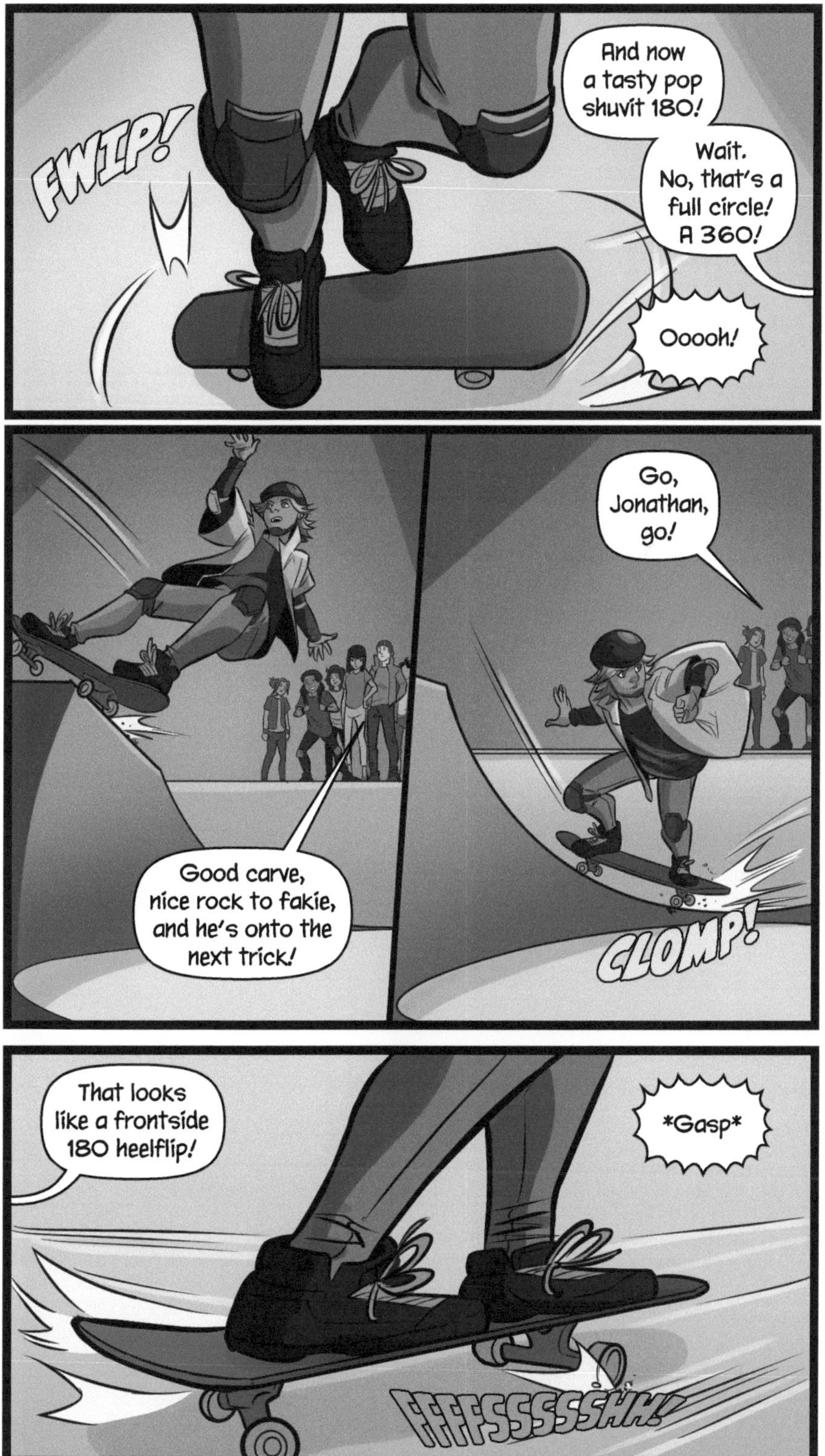

FWIP!
And now a tasty pop shuvit 180!
Wait. No, that's a full circle! A 360!
Ooooh!
Good carve, nice rock to fakie, and he's onto the next trick!
Go, Jonathan, go!
CLOMP!
That looks like a frontside 180 heelflip!
Gasp
FFFFSSSSSHH!

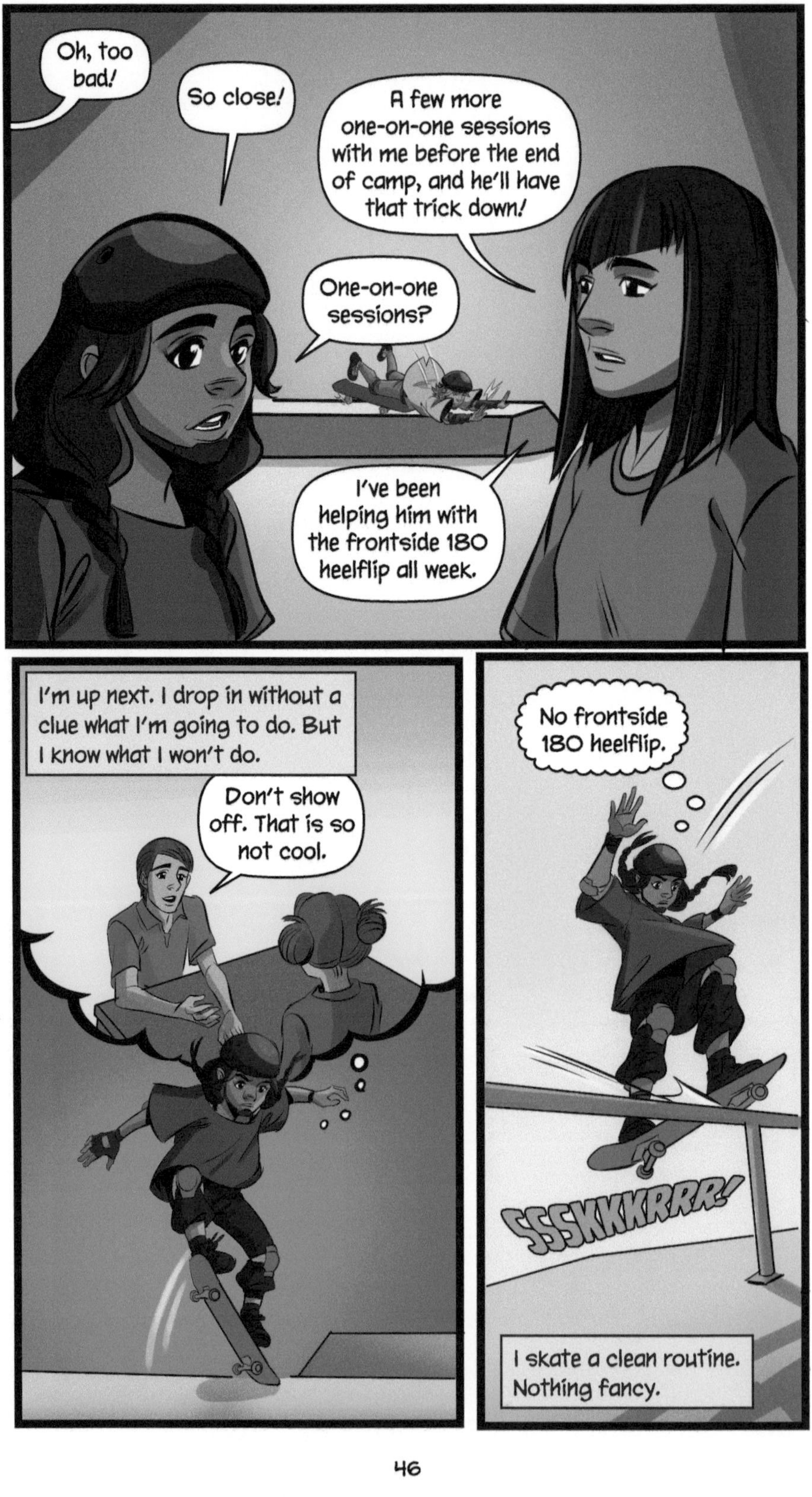
Oh, too bad!
So close!
A few more one-on-one sessions with me before the end of camp, and he'll have that trick down!
One-on-one sessions?
I've been helping him with the frontside 180 heelflip all week.
I'm up next. I drop in without a clue what I'm going to do. But I know what I won't do.
Don't show off. That is so not cool.
No frontside 180 heelflip.
SSSKKKRRR!
I skate a clean routine. Nothing fancy.

Kylie, Sunny, and Dawn keep it simple too. Simple, but good.

FWIP!

SSSKKRR!

WHOOOSH!

And Crash does a, um, something interesting.

Do you think we did enough to win?

Yeah, I think we did enough.

CLOP!

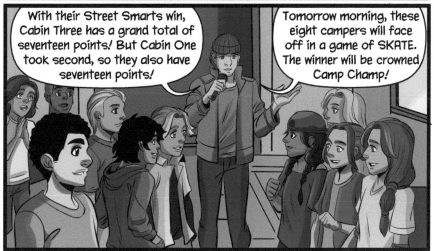

With their Street Smarts win, Cabin Three has a grand total of seventeen points! But Cabin One took second, so they also have seventeen points!

Tomorrow morning, these eight campers will face off in a game of SKATE. The winner will be crowned Camp Champ!

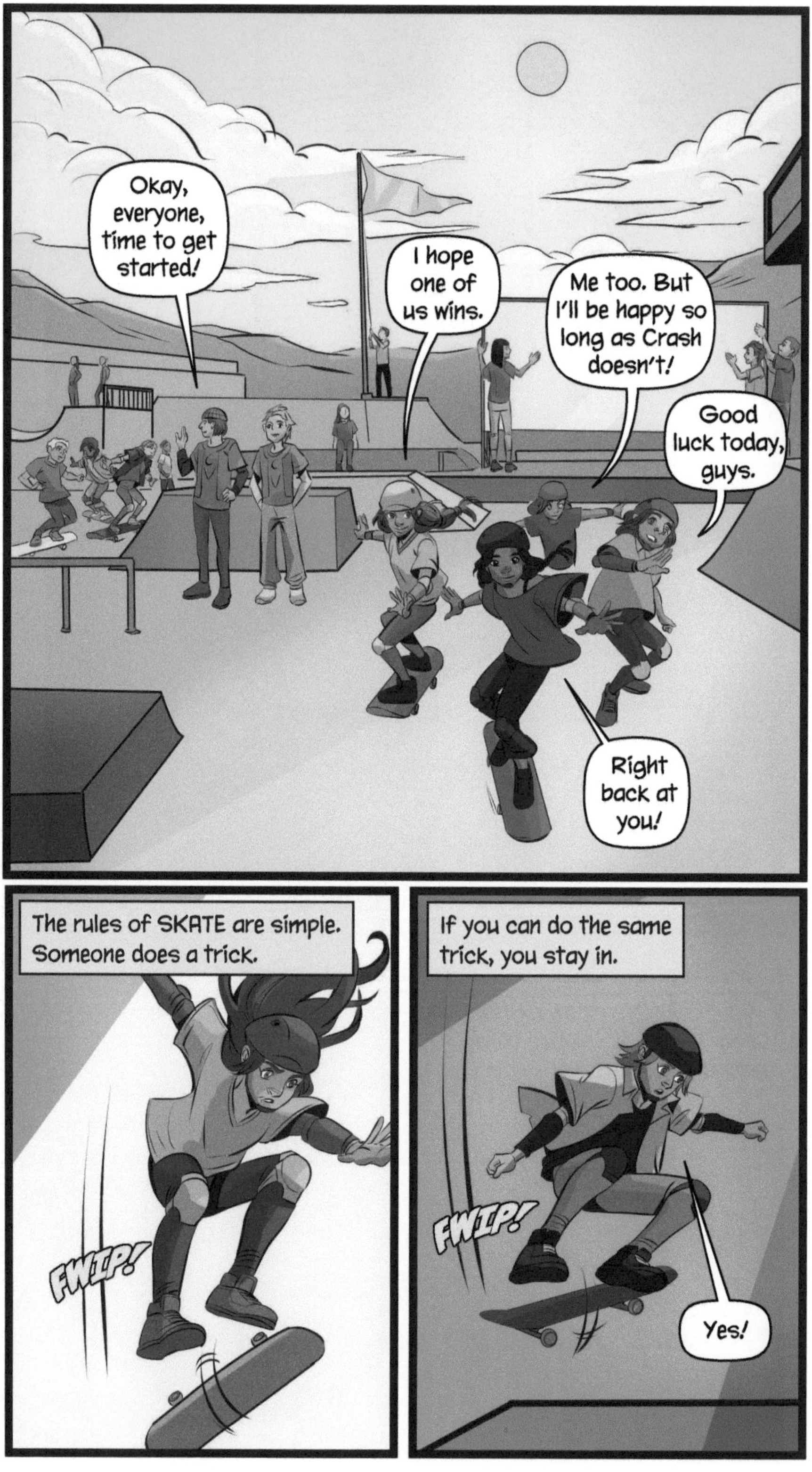
Okay, everyone, time to get started!
I hope one of us wins.
Me too. But I'll be happy so long as Crash doesn't!
Good luck today, guys.
Right back at you!
The rules of SKATE are simple. Someone does a trick.
FWIP!
If you can do the same trick, you stay in.
FWIP!
Yes!

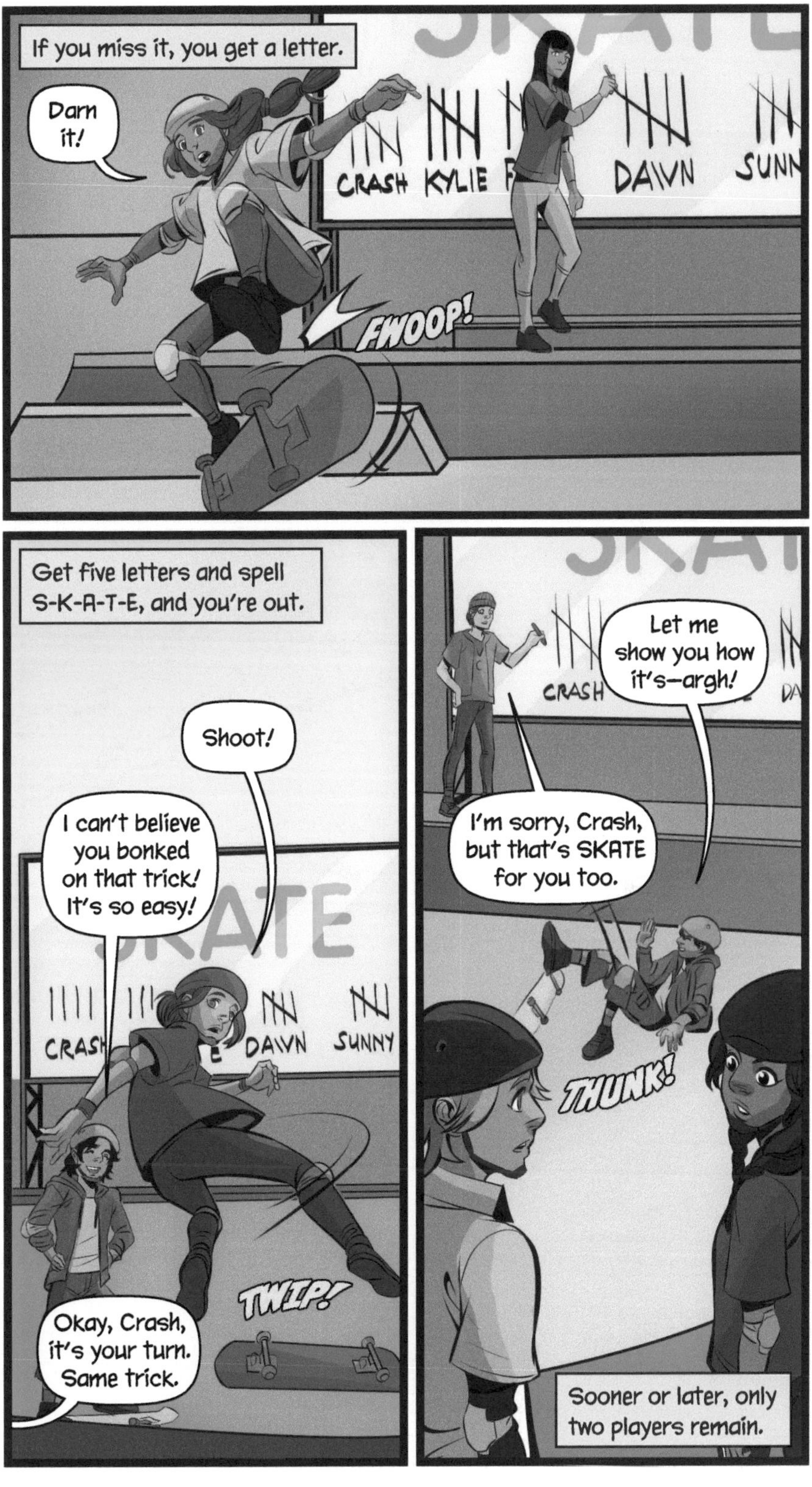

If you miss it, you get a letter.
Darn it!
CRASH KYLIE
DAWN SUNN
FWOOP!
Get five letters and spell S-K-A-T-E, and you're out.
Shoot!
I can't believe you bonked on that trick! It's so easy!
CRASH DAWN SUNNY
TWIP!
Okay, Crash, it's your turn. Same trick.
Let me show you how it's—argh!
CRASH
I'm sorry, Crash, but that's SKATE for you too.
THUNK!
Sooner or later, only two players remain.

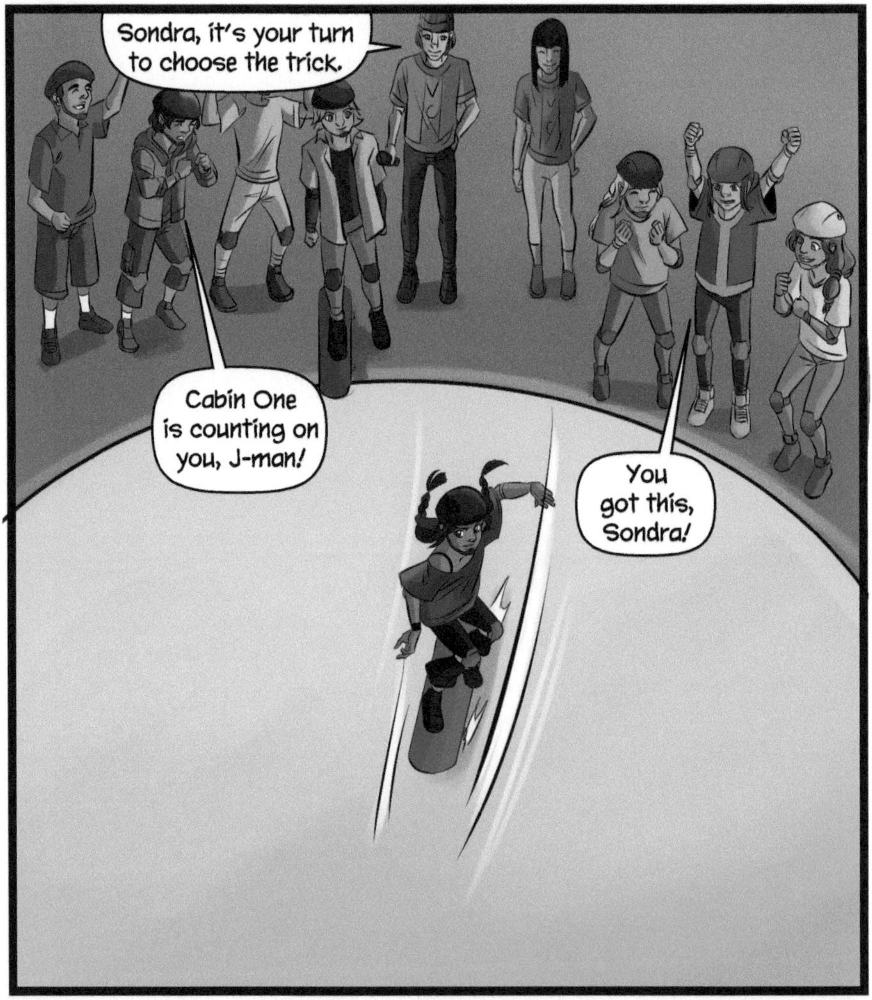
Sondra, it's your turn to choose the trick.
Cabin One is counting on you, J-man!
You got this, Sondra!

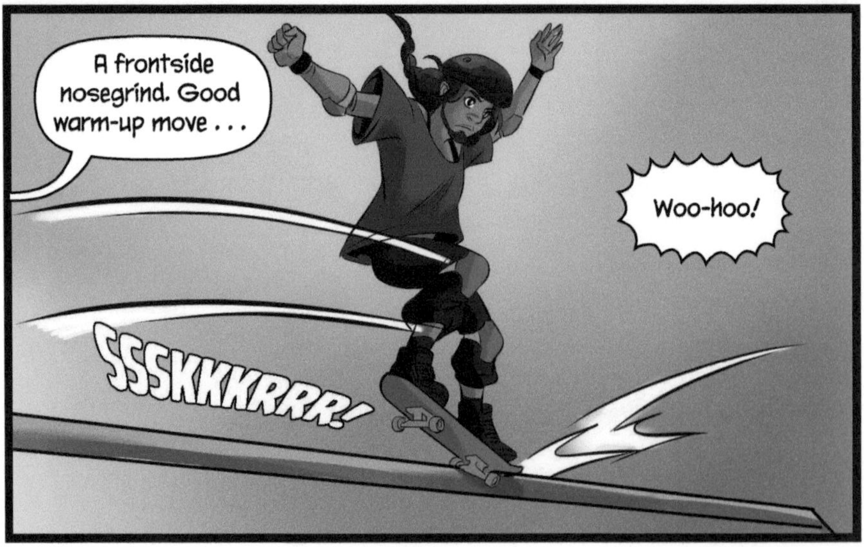
A frontside nosegrind. Good warm-up move . . .
Woo-hoo!
SSSKKKRRR!

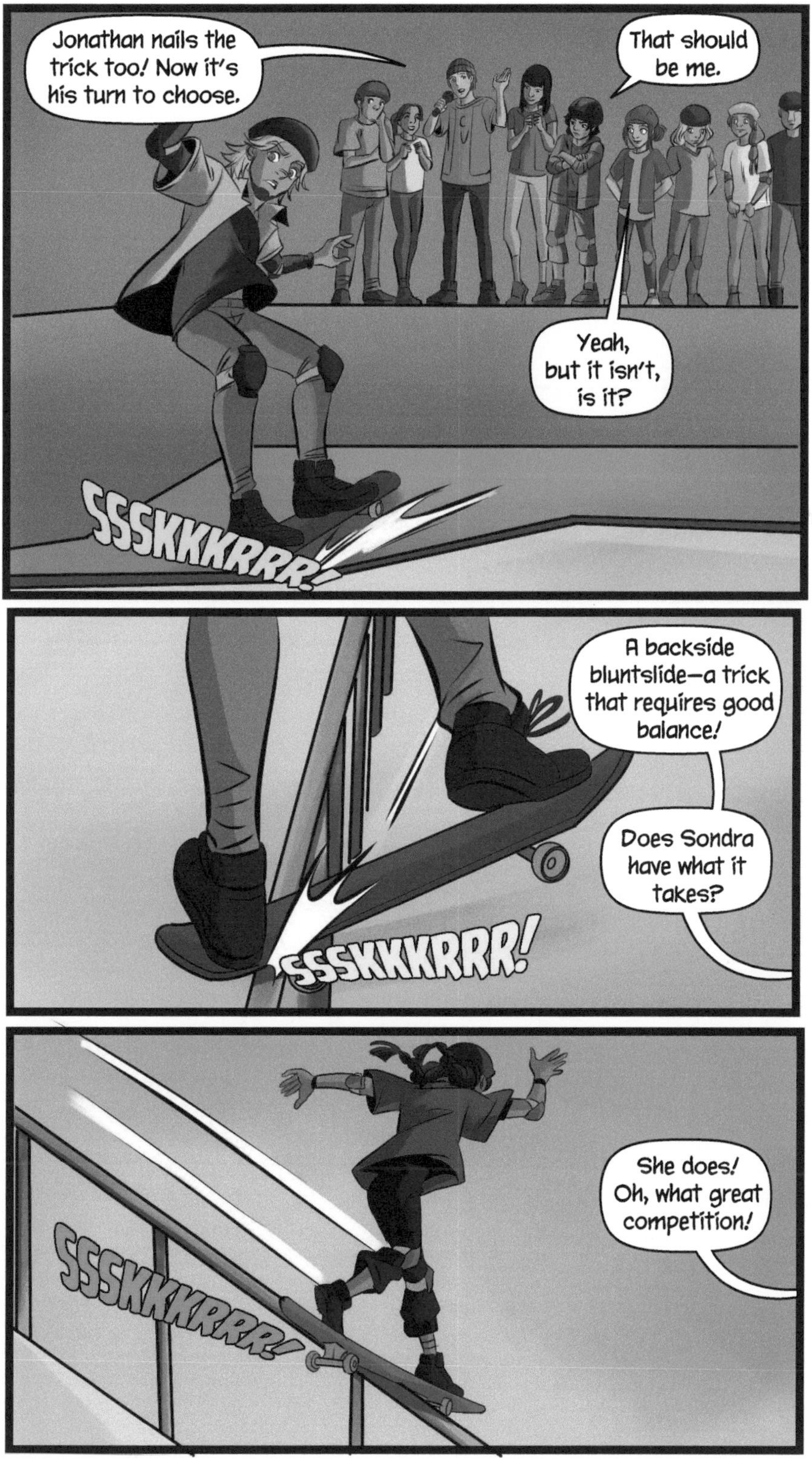
Jonathan nails the trick too! Now it's his turn to choose.
That should be me.
Yeah, but it isn't, is it?
SSSKKKRRR!
A backside bluntslide—a trick that requires good balance!
Does Sondra have what it takes?
SSSKKKRRR!
She does! Oh, what great competition!
SSSKKKRRR!

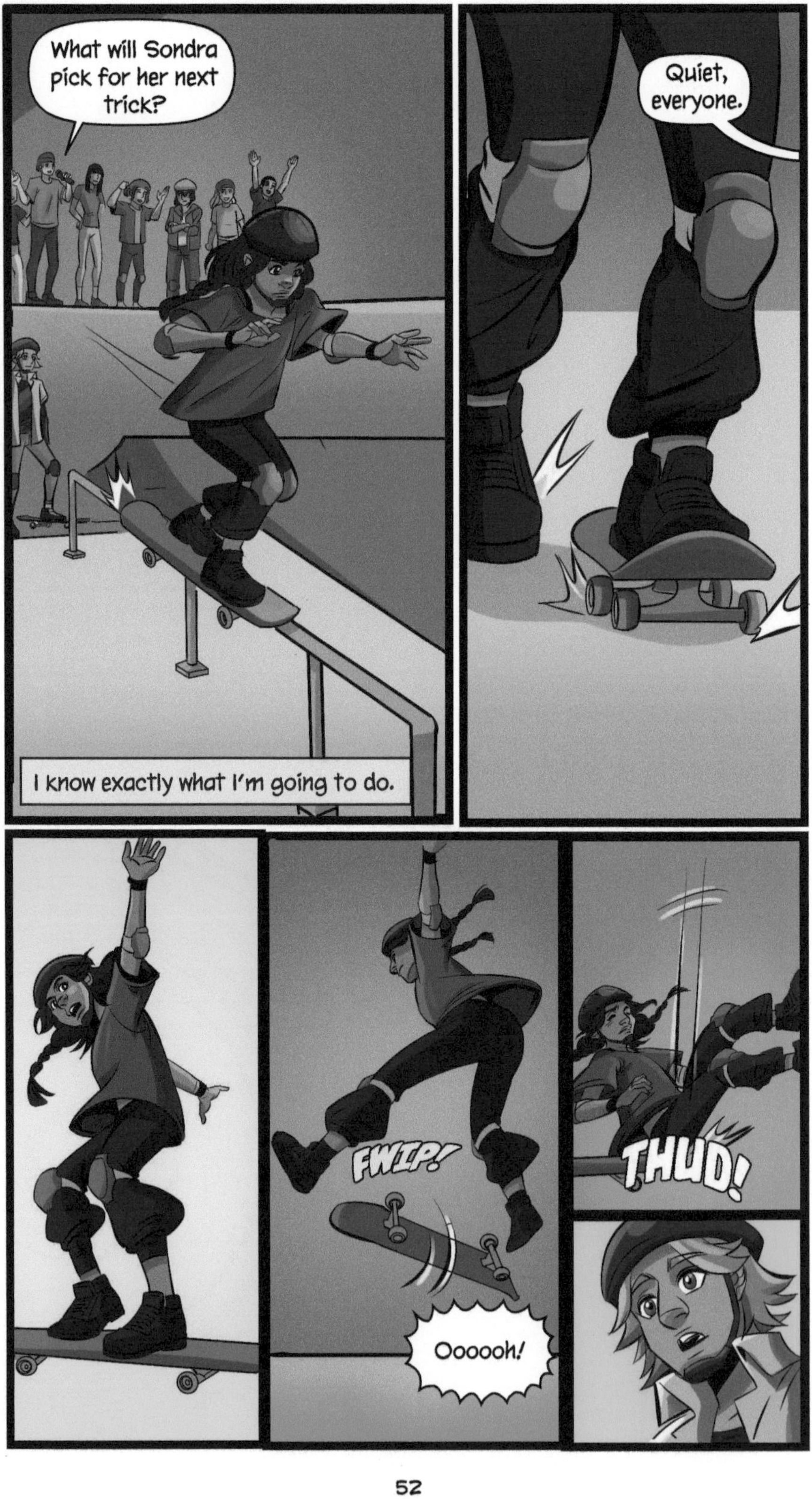
What will Sondra pick for her next trick?
I know exactly what I'm going to do.
Quiet, everyone.
FWIP!
Oooooh!
THUD!

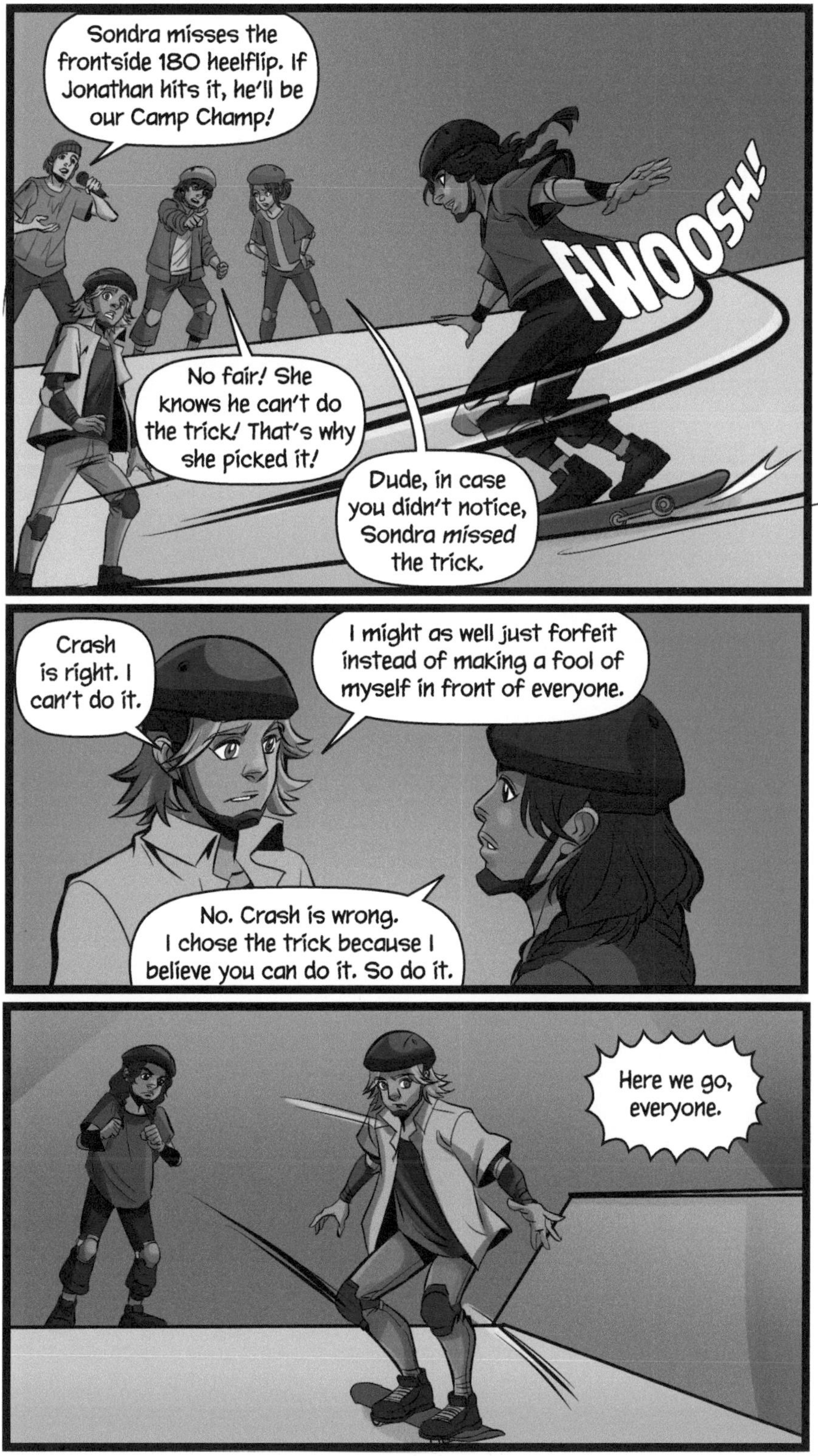
Sondra misses the frontside 180 heelflip. If Jonathan hits it, he'll be our Camp Champ!
FWOOSH!
No fair! She knows he can't do the trick! That's why she picked it!
Dude, in case you didn't notice, Sondra *missed* the trick.
Crash is right. I can't do it.
I might as well just forfeit instead of making a fool of myself in front of everyone.
No. Crash is wrong. I chose the trick because I believe you can do it. So do it.
Here we go, everyone.

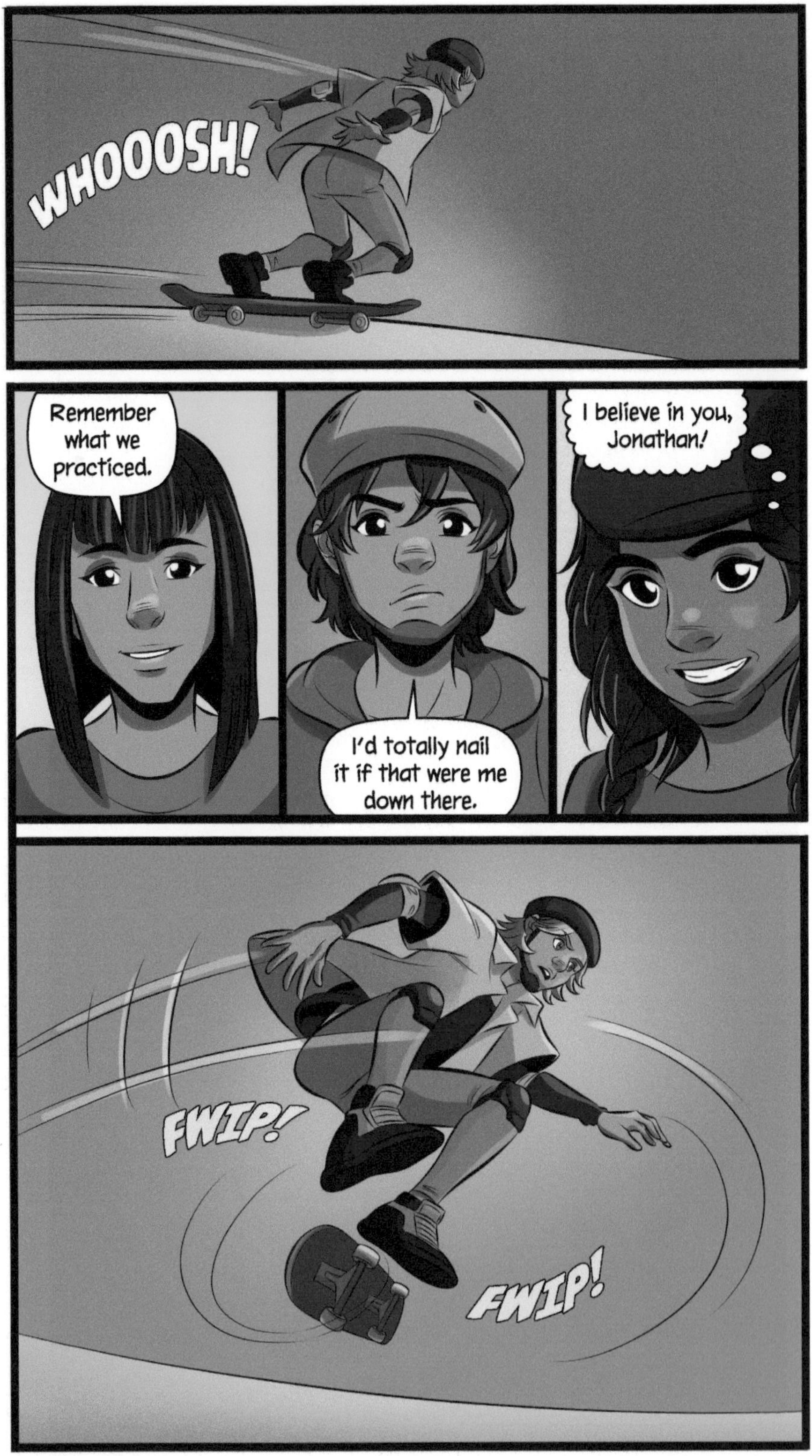
WHOOOSH!
Remember what we practiced.
I'd totally nail it if that were me down there.
I believe in you, Jonathan!
FWIP!
FWIP!

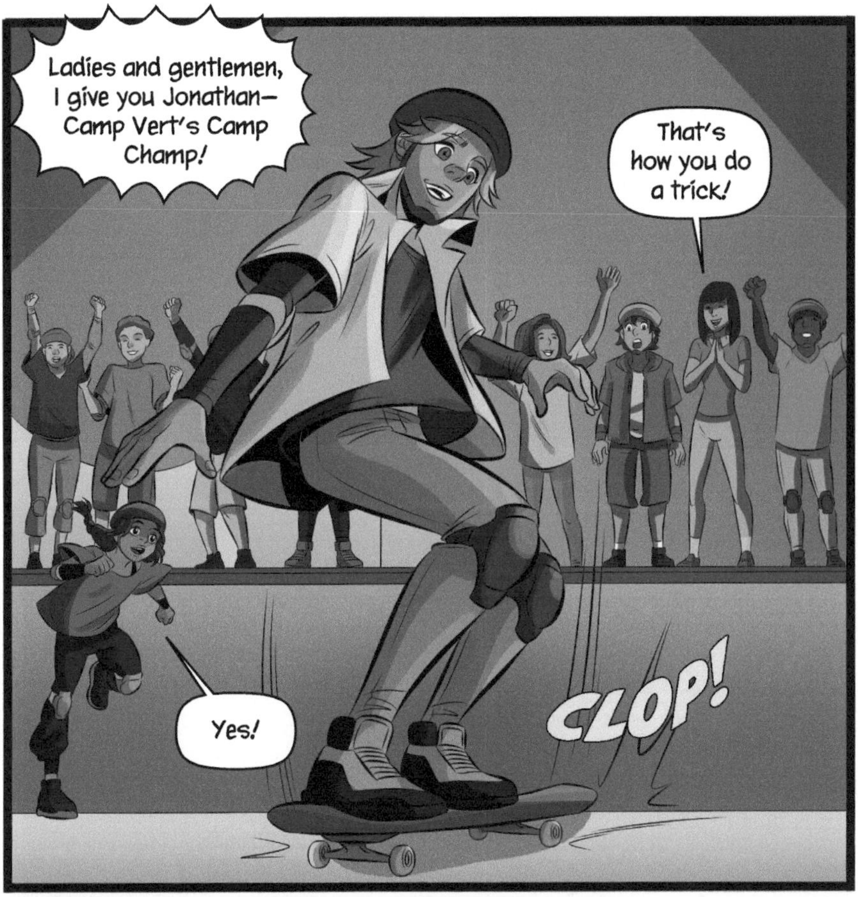
Ladies and gentlemen, I give you Jonathan—Camp Vert's Camp Champ!
That's how you do a trick!
Yes!
CLOP!

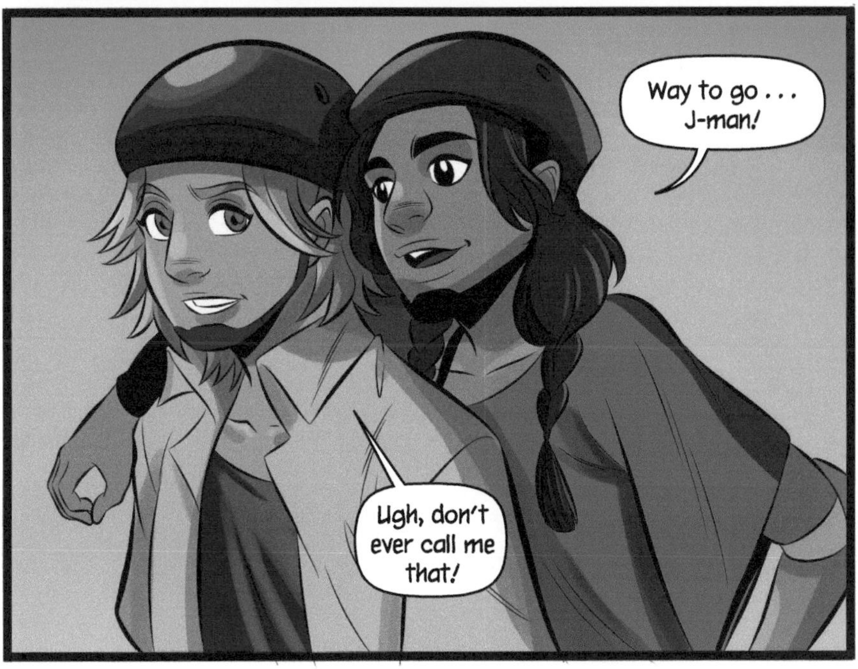
Way to go . . . J-man!
Ugh, don't ever call me that!

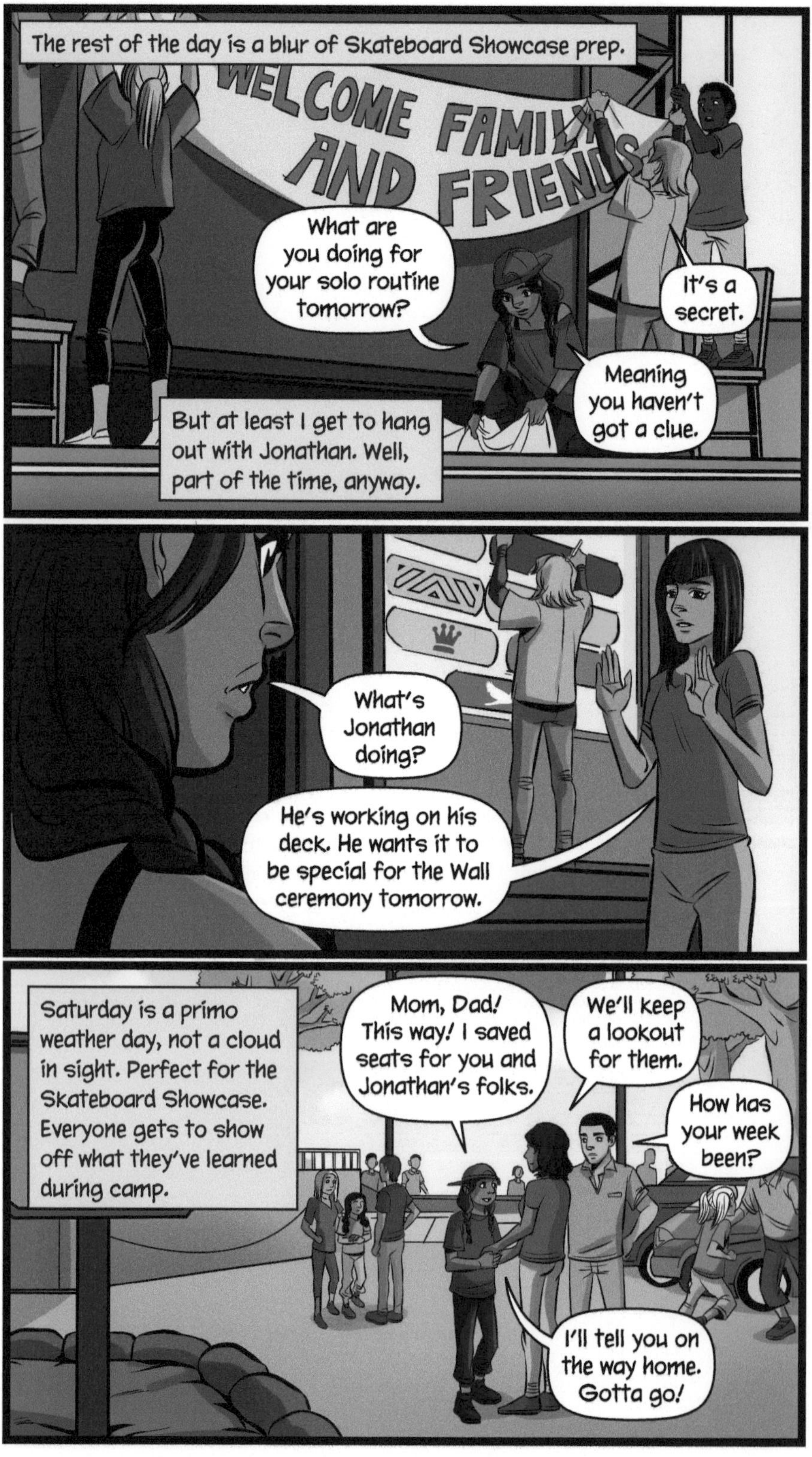
The rest of the day is a blur of Skateboard Showcase prep.
WELCOME FAMILIES AND FRIENDS
What are you doing for your solo routine tomorrow?
It's a secret.
Meaning you haven't got a clue.
But at least I get to hang out with Jonathan. Well, part of the time, anyway.
What's Jonathan doing?
He's working on his deck. He wants it to be special for the Wall ceremony tomorrow.
Saturday is a primo weather day, not a cloud in sight. Perfect for the Skateboard Showcase. Everyone gets to show off what they've learned during camp.
Mom, Dad! This way! I saved seats for you and Jonathan's folks.
We'll keep a lookout for them.
How has your week been?
I'll tell you on the way home. Gotta go!

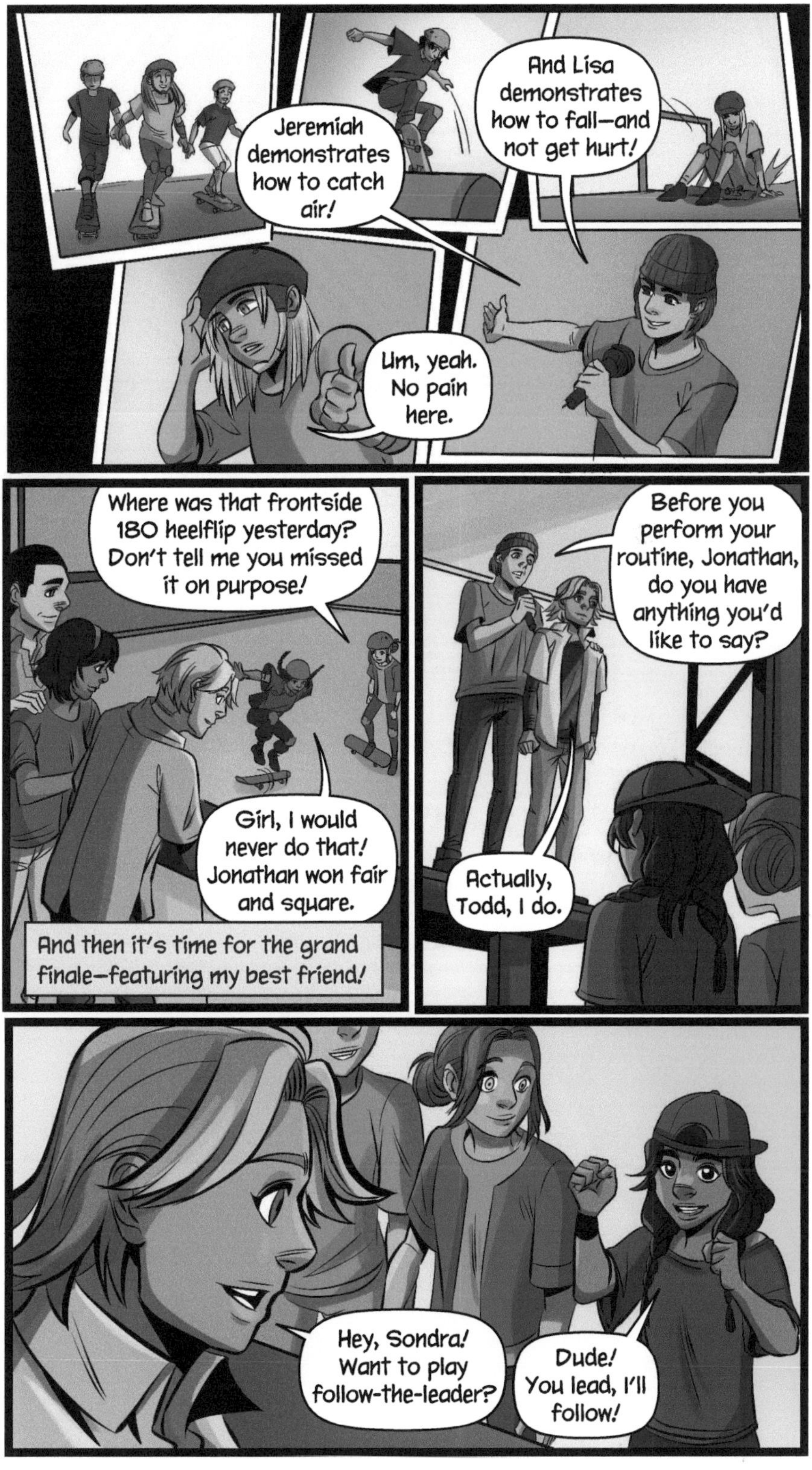
Jeremiah demonstrates how to catch air!
And Lisa demonstrates how to fall—and not get hurt!
Um, yeah. No pain here.
Where was that frontside 180 heelflip yesterday? Don't tell me you missed it on purpose!
Girl, I would never do that! Jonathan won fair and square.
And then it's time for the grand finale—featuring my best friend!
Before you perform your routine, Jonathan, do you have anything you'd like to say?
Actually, Todd, I do.
Hey, Sondra! Want to play follow-the-leader?
Dude! You lead, I'll follow!

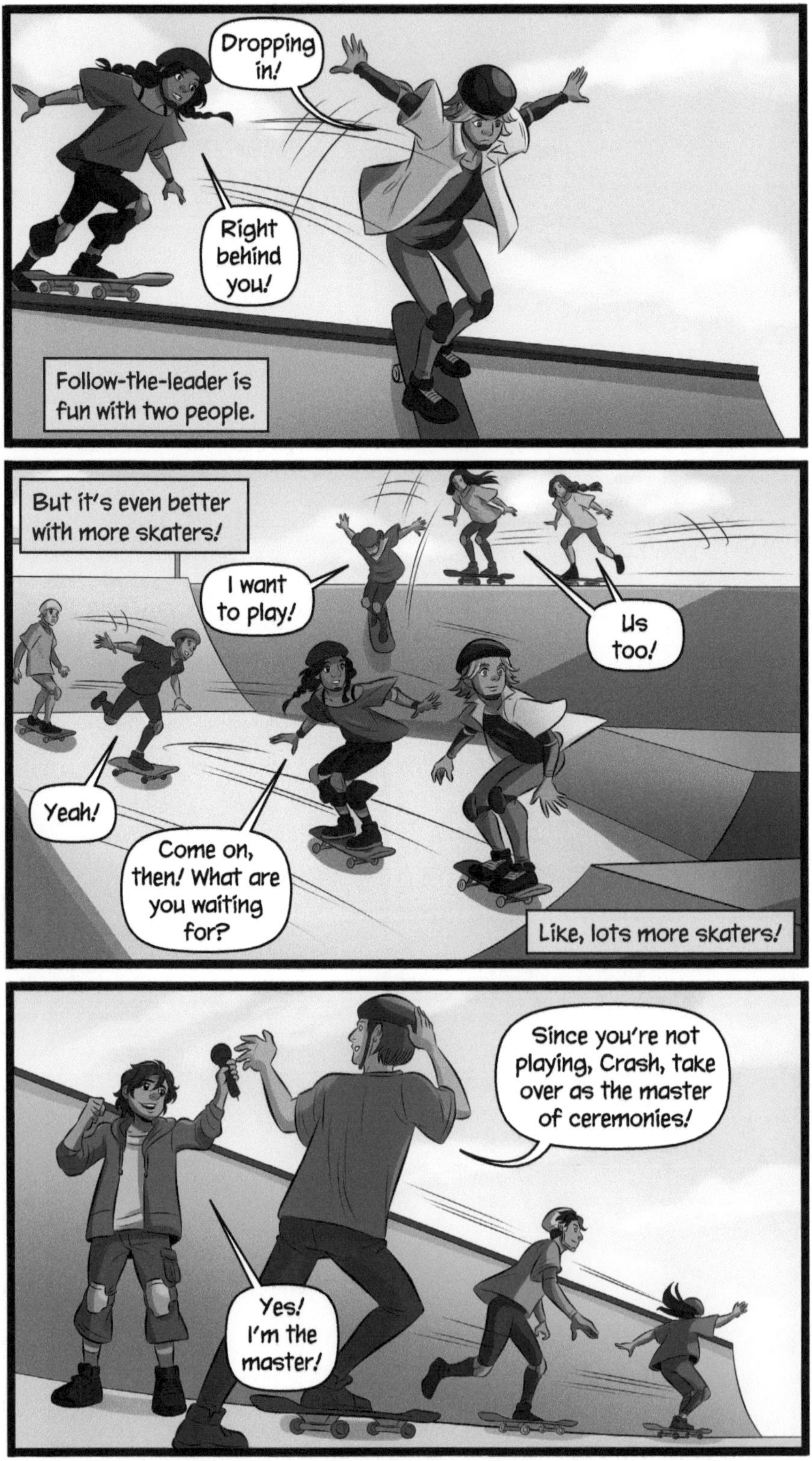
Dropping in!
Right behind you!
Follow-the-leader is fun with two people.
But it's even better with more skaters!
I want to play!
Us too!
Yeah!
Come on, then! What are you waiting for?
Like, lots more skaters!
Since you're not playing, Crash, take over as the master of ceremonies!
Yes! I'm the master!

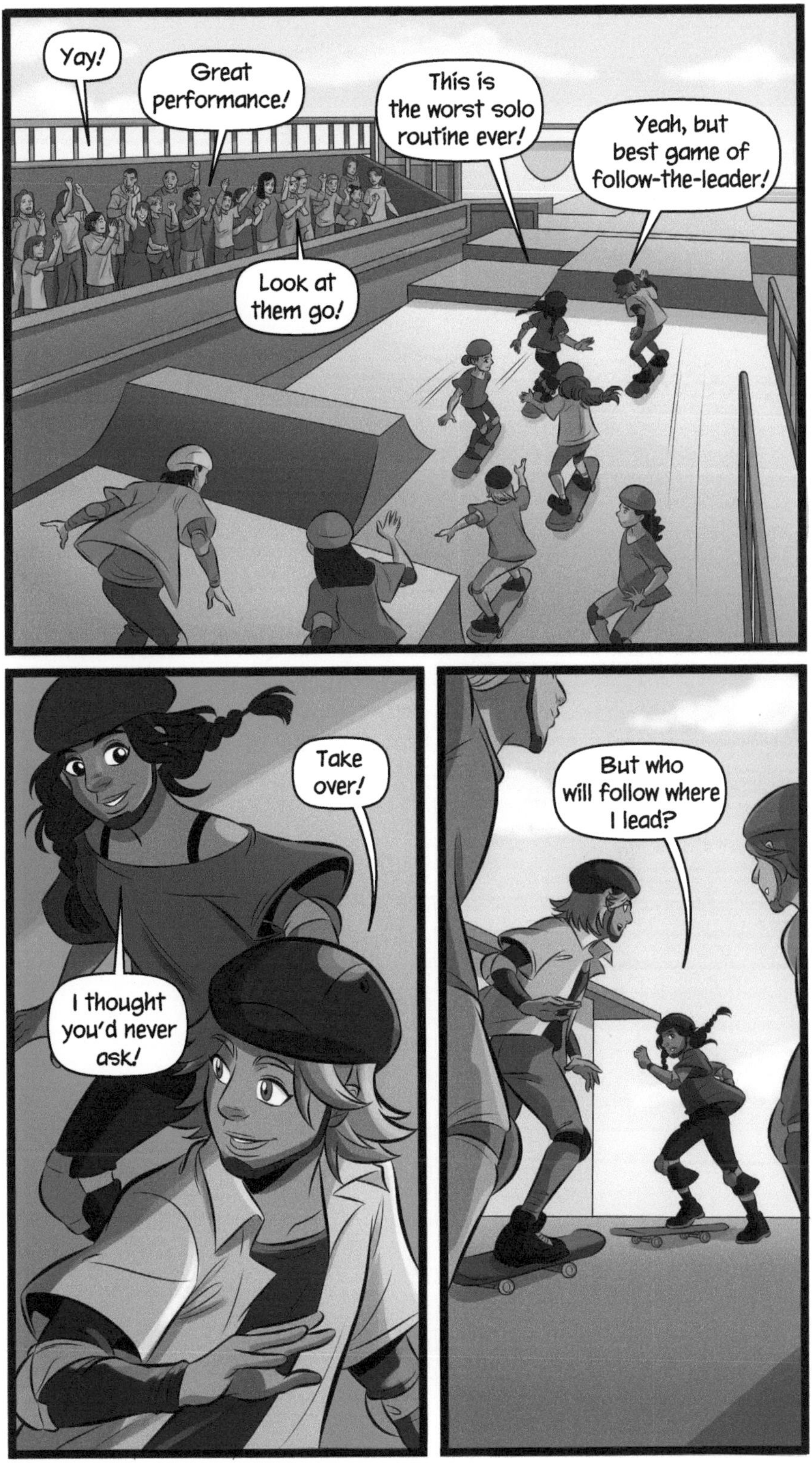
Yay!
Great performance!
Look at them go!
This is the worst solo routine ever!
Yeah, but best game of follow-the-leader!
Take over!
I thought you'd never ask!
But who will follow where I lead?

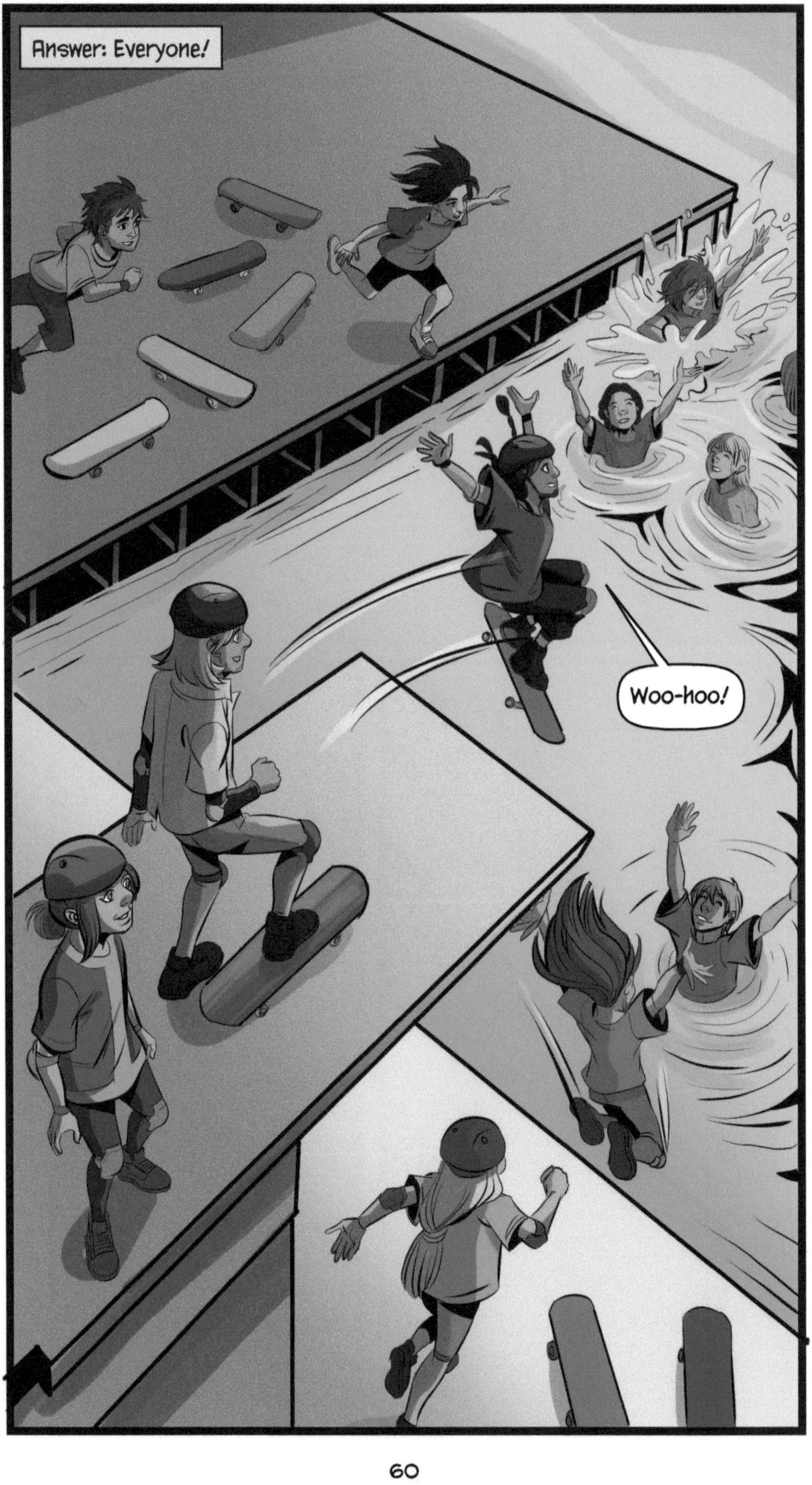
Answer: Everyone!
Woo-hoo!

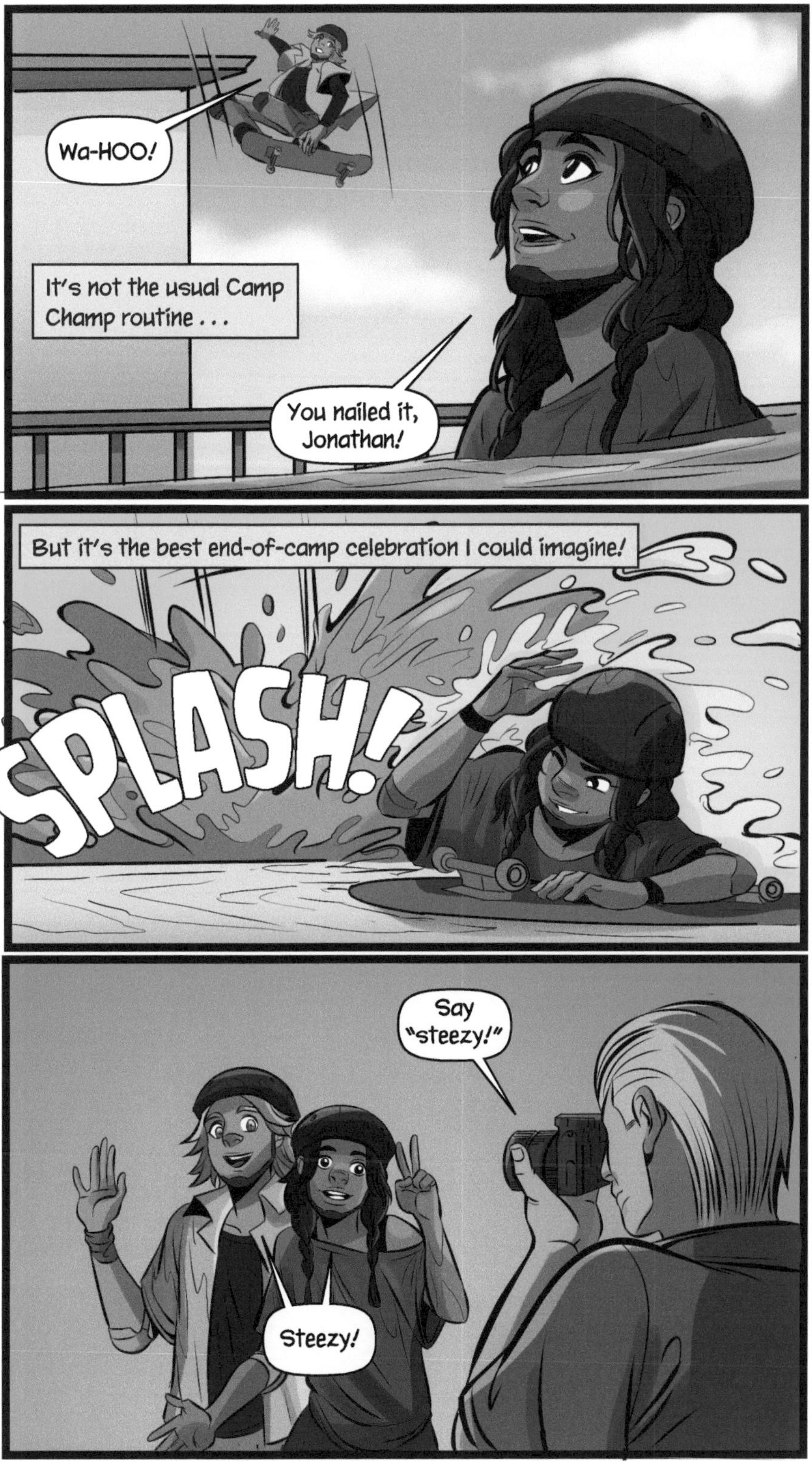

Wa-HOO!
It's not the usual Camp Champ routine . . .
You nailed it, Jonathan!
But it's the best end-of-camp celebration I could imagine!
SPLASH!
Say "steezy!"
Steezy!

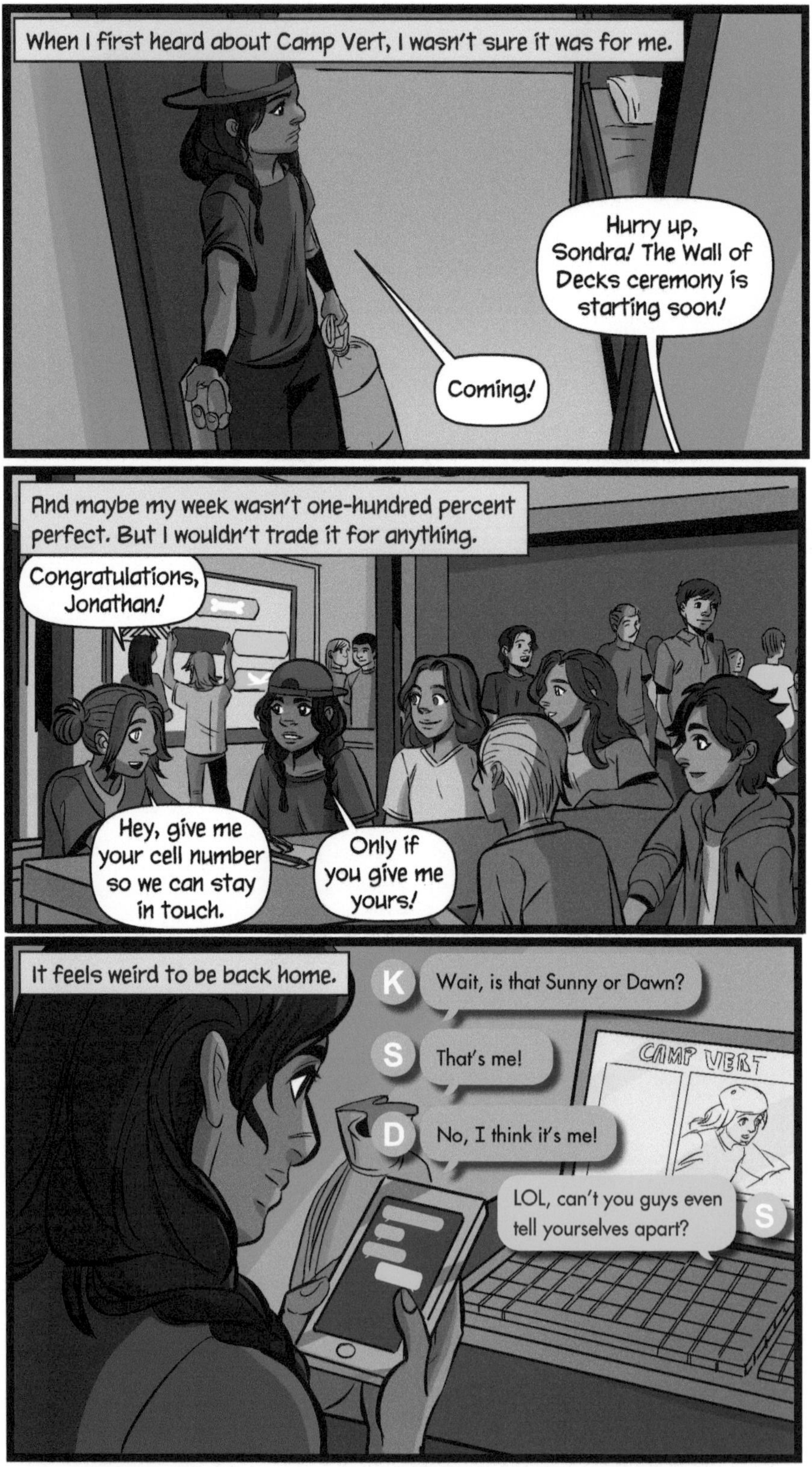
When I first heard about Camp Vert, I wasn't sure it was for me.
Hurry up, Sondra! The Wall of Decks ceremony is starting soon!
Coming!
And maybe my week wasn't one-hundred percent perfect. But I wouldn't trade it for anything.
Congratulations, Jonathan!
Hey, give me your cell number so we can stay in touch.
Only if you give me yours!
It feels weird to be back home.
K
Wait, is that Sunny or Dawn?
S
That's me!
D
No, I think it's me!
LOL, can't you guys even tell yourselves apart?
S
CAMP VERT

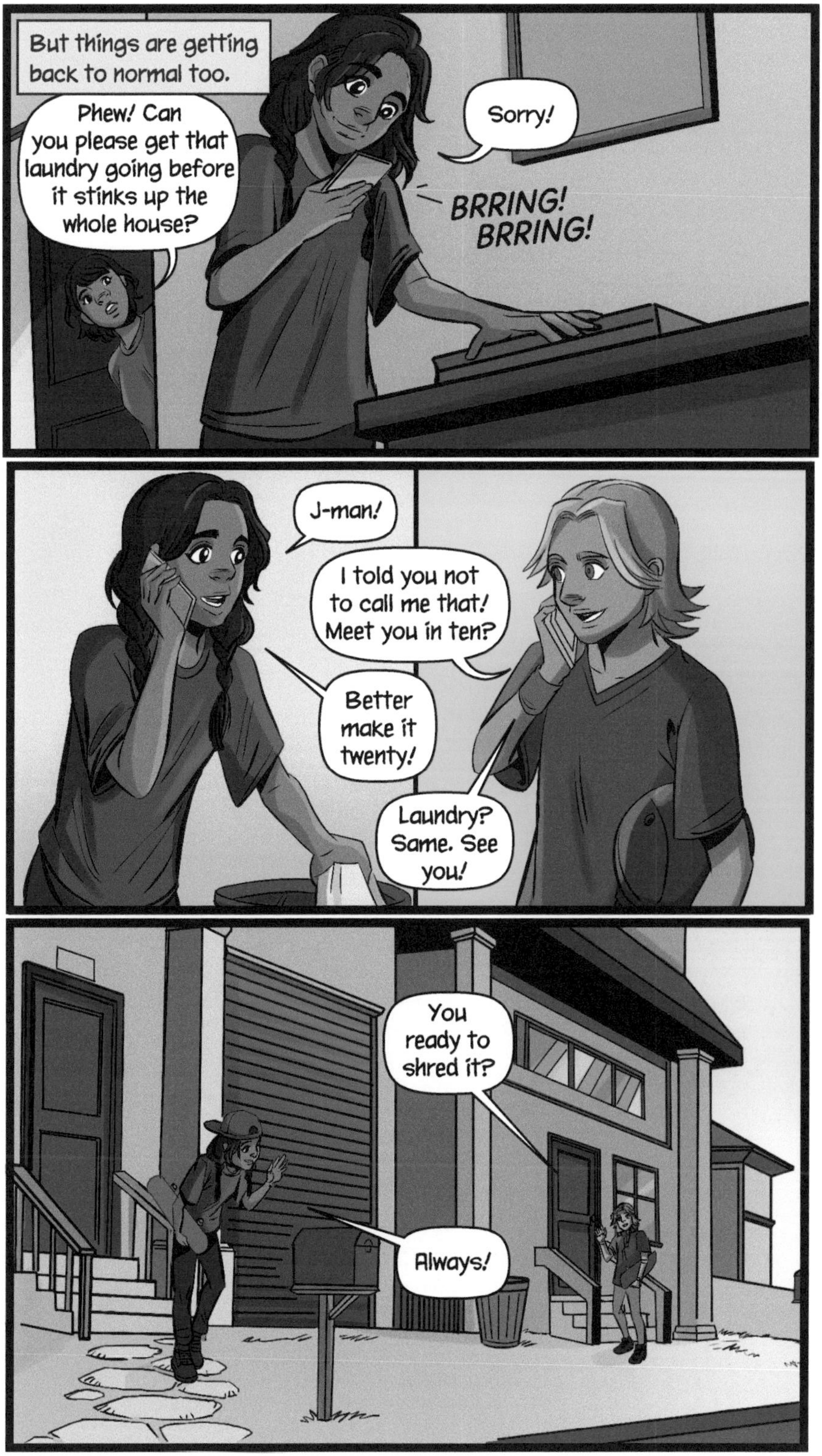

But things are getting back to normal too.
Phew! Can you please get that laundry going before it stinks up the whole house?
Sorry!
BRRING! BRRING!
J-man!
I told you not to call me that! Meet you in ten?
Better make it twenty!
Laundry? Same. See you!
You ready to shred it?
Always!

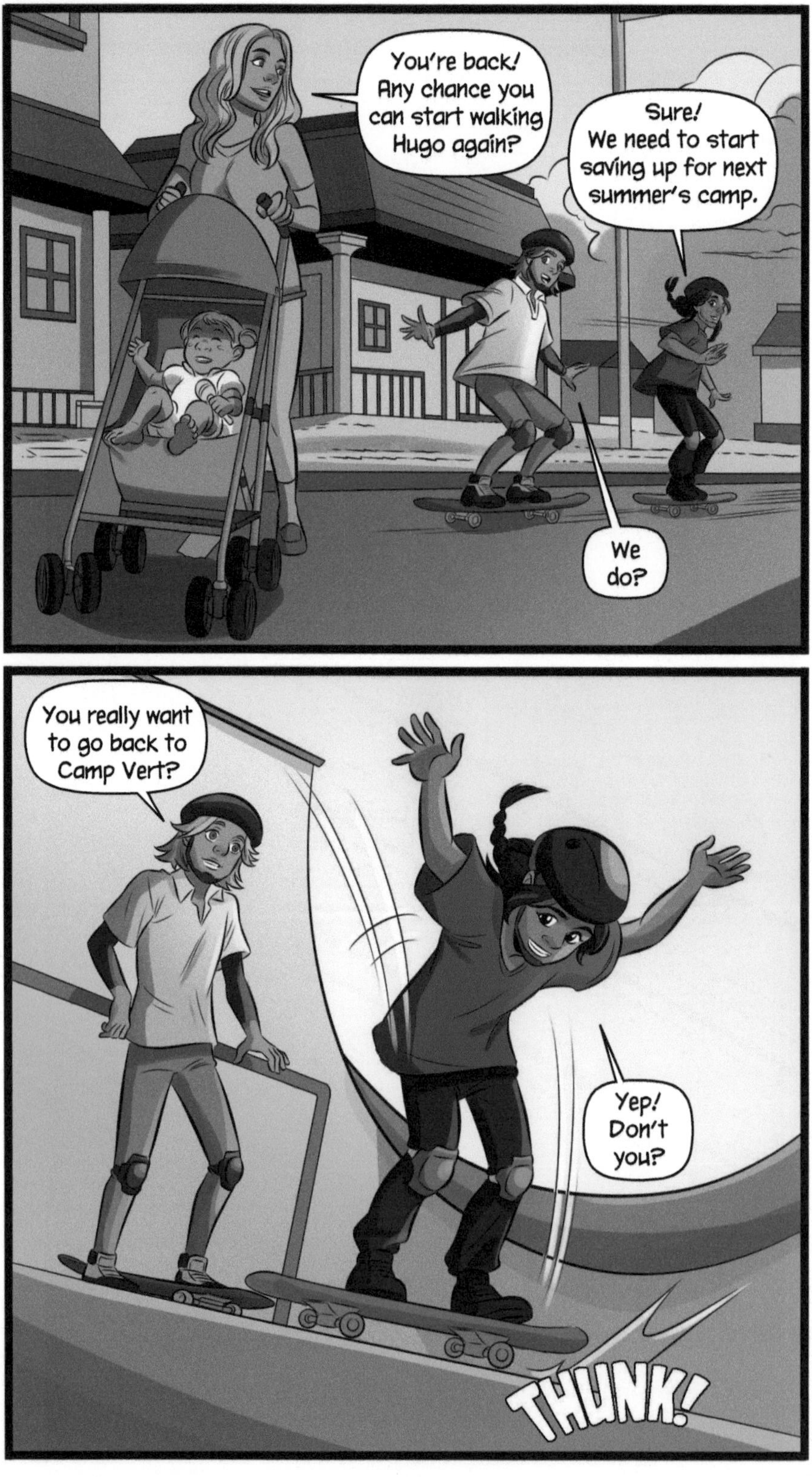
You're back! Any chance you can start walking Hugo again?
Sure! We need to start saving up for next summer's camp.
We do?
You really want to go back to Camp Vert?
Yep! Don't you?
THUNK!

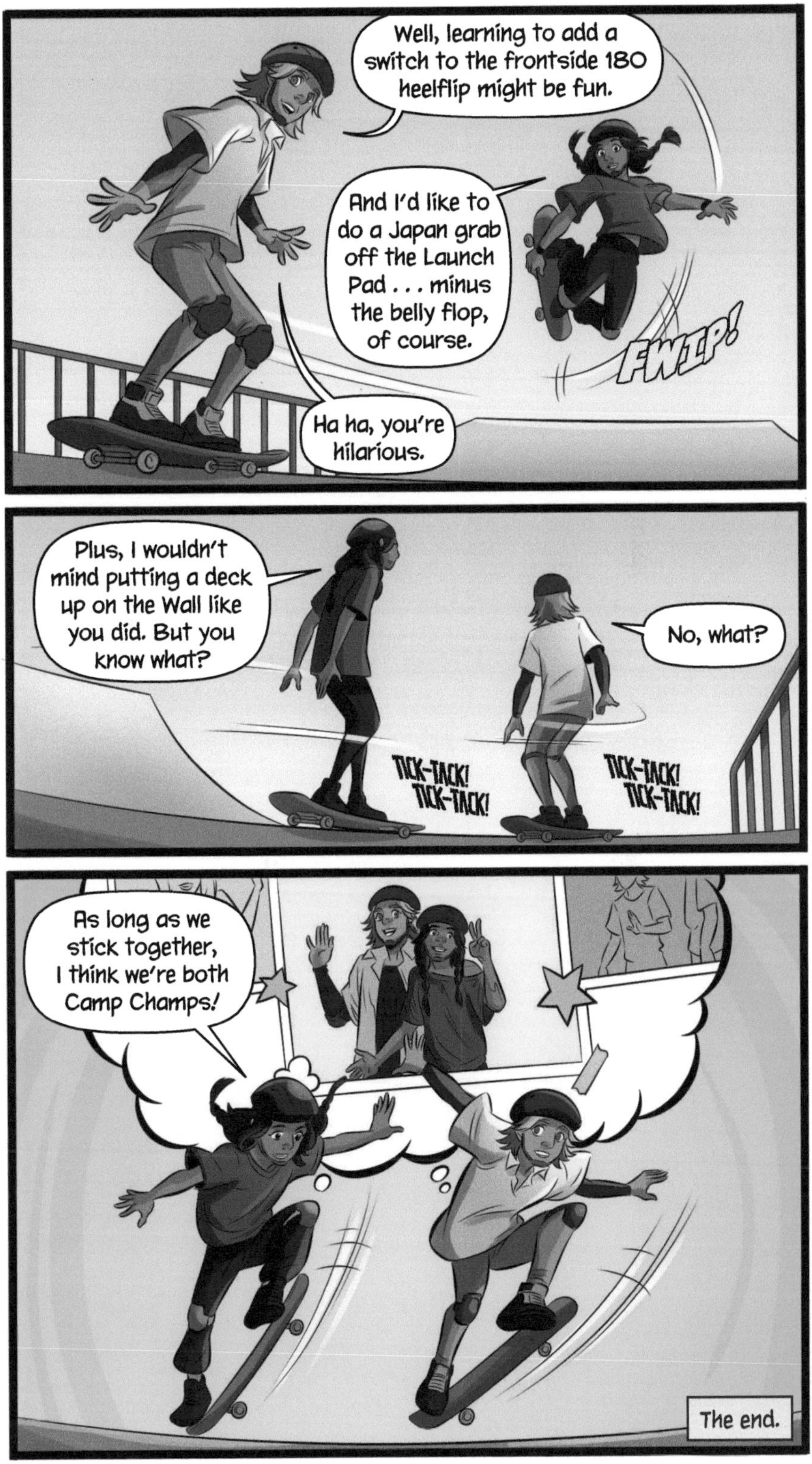
Well, learning to add a switch to the frontside 180 heelflip might be fun.
And I'd like to do a Japan grab off the Launch Pad . . . minus the belly flop, of course.
FWIP!
Ha ha, you're hilarious.
Plus, I wouldn't mind putting a deck up on the Wall like you did. But you know what?
No, what?
TICK-TACK! TICK-TACK!
TICK-TACK! TICK-TACK!
As long as we stick together, I think we're both Camp Champs!
The end.

VISUAL QUESTIONS

1. Study the above panel. What is the artist trying to show? Is there anything special about the panel that shows when this scene takes place?

2. This panel shows several images. Why do you think the artist chose this method to show several scenes from the competition?

3. Closeup shots help us see what a character is thinking or feeling during the story. What is Jonathan feeling in this closeup?

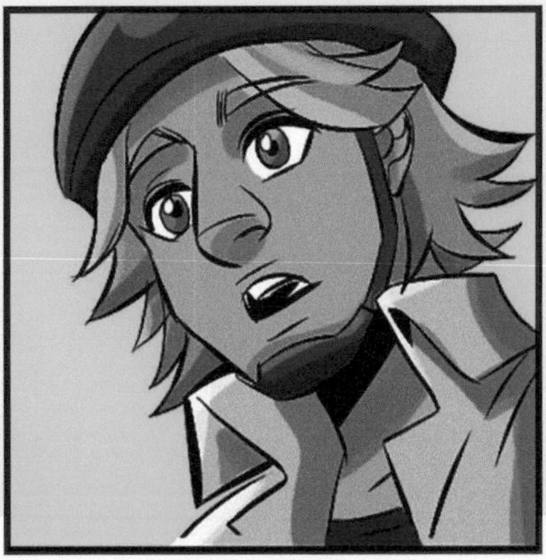

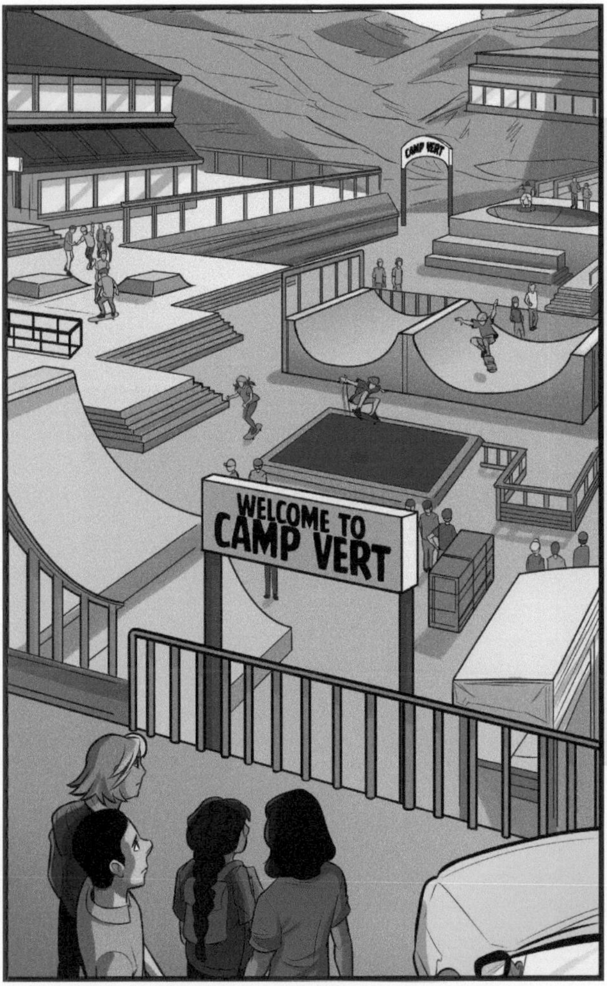
CAMP VERT
WELCOME TO CAMP VERT

4. Large panels often give readers a good view of the location where a story takes place. Study this large scene of Camp Vert. How many different skating features can you find?

LEARN THE SKATEBOARDING TERMS

50-50 axle stall—a stall on both trucks of a skateboard

benihana—a trick where one hand grabs the tail of the board and the back foot is released from the board

bluntslide—a trick where the skater performs an ollie onto a rail and catches only the tail of the board under the rear trucks

deck—the flat board that you stand on when skating

fakie—a movement in which the board is ridden backward

goofy foot—riding with the left foot in back, toward the tail of the board

grab—using either hand to hold the deck during an aerial trick

grind—trick that involves the skateboarder sliding along a surface with the trucks making contact with the obstacle

heelflip—a trick where the skateboarder kicks out and flips the board 360 degrees along the board's long axis, rotating on the toe-side of the skateboard

kickflip—a trick where the skateboarder kicks out and flips the board 360 degrees along the board's long axis, rotating on the heel-side of the skateboard

lipslide—a slide where the tail of the board goes over the obstacle with the board sliding between the two trucks

nollie—short for "nose ollie"; an ollie performed at the front of the board where the rider is positioned in their natural stance

nosegrind—a trick where the skater grinds on a ledge using only the front truck of the skateboard

ollie—a trick where the rider and skateboard leap into the air without the use of the rider's hands

pop shuvit—a trick where the rider uses their back foot to pop and spin the skateboard in the air

snaking—taking a run when another skater is already using the obstacle

switch—riding in the opposite direction than usual

truck—the metal piece mounted to the bottom of the skateboard to keep the wheels attached to the deck

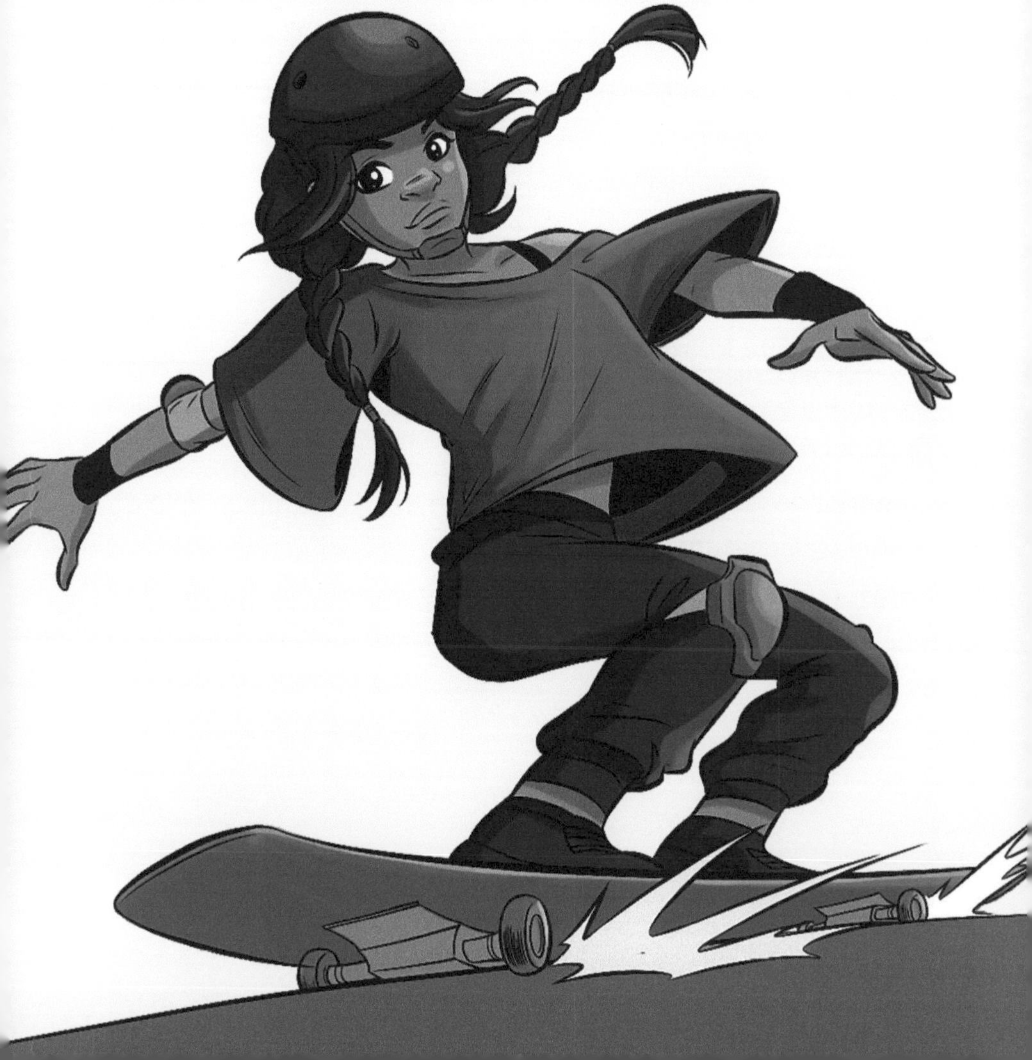

GLOSSARY

bunkmate (BUHNGK-mate)—a person who sleeps in the same area as another

competition (kahm-puh-TI-shuhn)—a contest between rivals or opposing teams

counselor (KOUN-suh-lur)—a person who is in charge of young people at a summer camp

demonstrate (DEM-uhn-strayt)—to show other people how to do something or use something

exhibition (ek-suh-BI-shuhn)—a public display where athletes show off their skills

face-plant (FASE-plant)—a sudden face-first fall

finale (fuh-NAL-ee)—the last part of a show

forfeit (FOR-fuht)—to give up the right to something

hilarious (hi-LAIR-ee-uhs)—very funny

routine (roo-TEEN)—a series of tricks linked one after another in a performance

trampoline (tram-puh-LEEN)—a piece of canvas attached to a frame by elastic ropes or springs

trash-talk (TRASH-tawk)—to talk in an insulting way about someone

ABOUT THE AUTHOR

Stephanie True Peters has been writing books for young readers for more than twenty-five years. Among her most recent titles are *Sleeping Beauty: Magic Master* and *Johnny Slimeseed*, both for Capstone's Far-Out Fairy Tale/Folk Tale series. An avid reader, workout enthusiast, and beach wanderer, Stephanie enjoys spending time with her children, Jackson and Chloe, her husband, Dan, and the family's two cats and two rabbits. She lives and works in Mansfield, Massachusetts.

ABOUT THE ARTISTS

Mel Joy San Juan is a full-time illustrator from Cavite, Philippines. She started illustrating various comic books and manga upon joining Glasshouse Graphics during her teenage years. She is best known for her graphic novel illustrations, such as Sherrilyn Kenyon's Dark Hunter series, the Call of Duty: Black Ops series for Activision, and other independent comic books. She is currently happily working on a comic book with the help of her sidekick, Maddie.

Berenice Muñiz is a graphic designer and illustrator from Monterrey, Mexico. She has done work for publicity agencies, art exhibitions, and even created her own webcomic. These days, Berenice is devoted to illustrating comics as part of the Graphikslava crew.

READ THEM ALL!

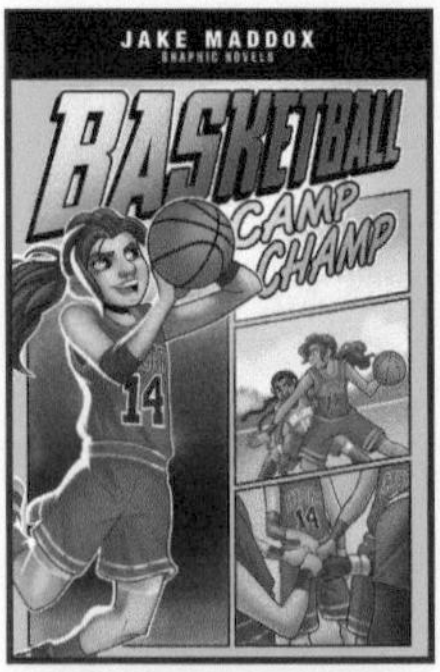
JAKE MADDOX
GRAPHIC NOVELS
BASKETBALL CAMP CHAMP

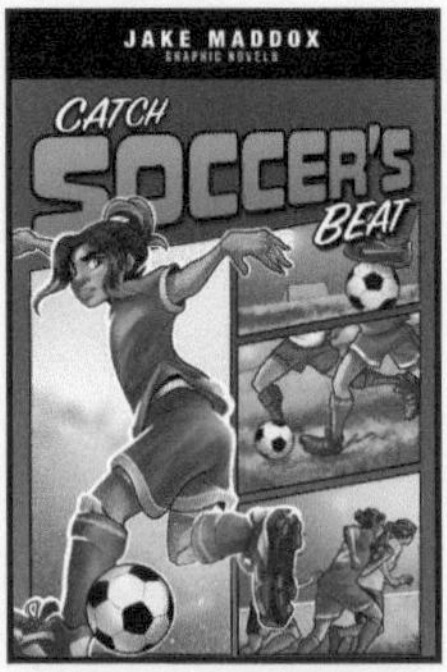
JAKE MADDOX
GRAPHIC NOVELS
CATCH SOCCER'S BEAT

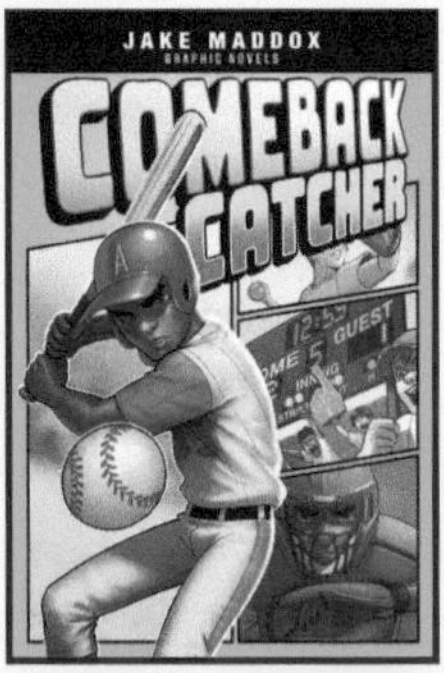
JAKE MADDOX
GRAPHIC NOVELS
COMEBACK CATCHER

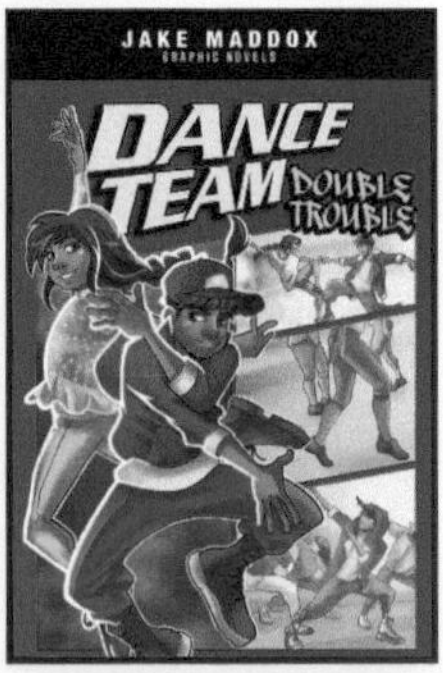
JAKE MADDOX
GRAPHIC NOVELS
DANCE TEAM DOUBLE TROUBLE

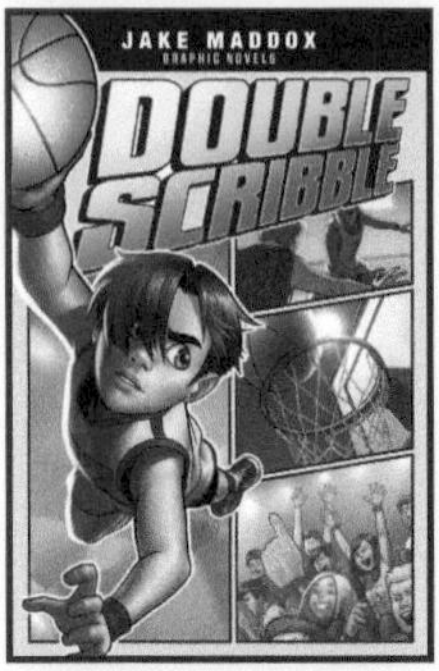
JAKE MADDOX
GRAPHIC NOVELS
DOUBLE SCRIBBLE

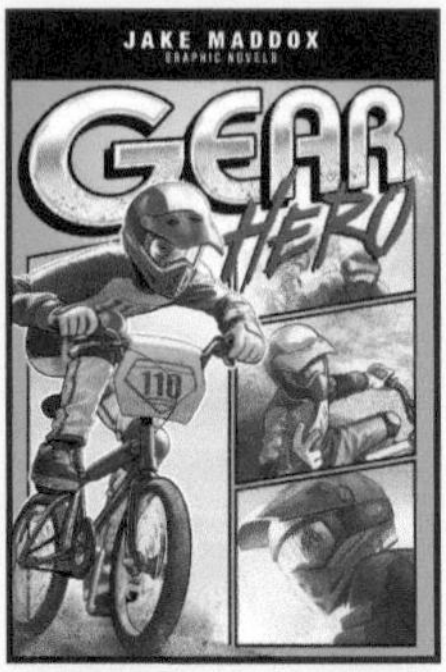
JAKE MADDOX
GRAPHIC NOVELS
GEAR HERO

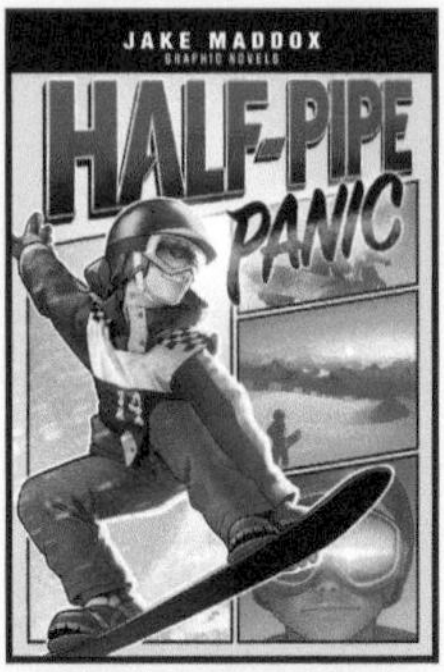
JAKE MADDOX
GRAPHIC NOVELS
HALF-PIPE PANIC

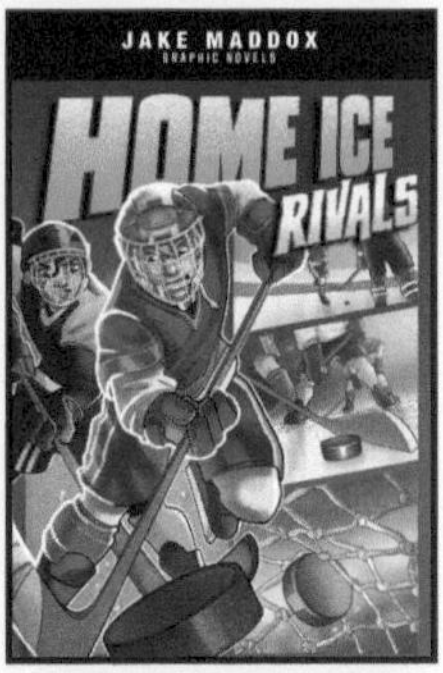
JAKE MADDOX
GRAPHIC NOVELS
HOME ICE RIVALS

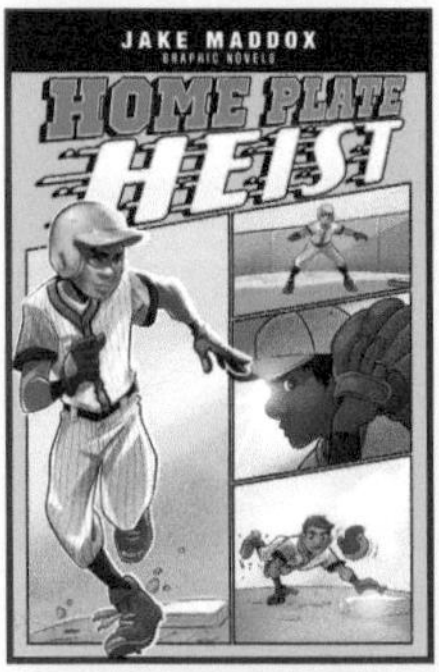
JAKE MADDOX
GRAPHIC NOVELS
HOME PLATE HEIST

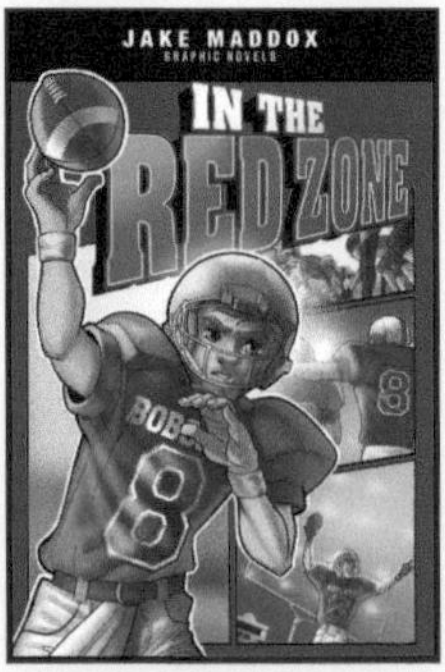
JAKE MADDOX
GRAPHIC NOVELS
IN THE RED ZONE

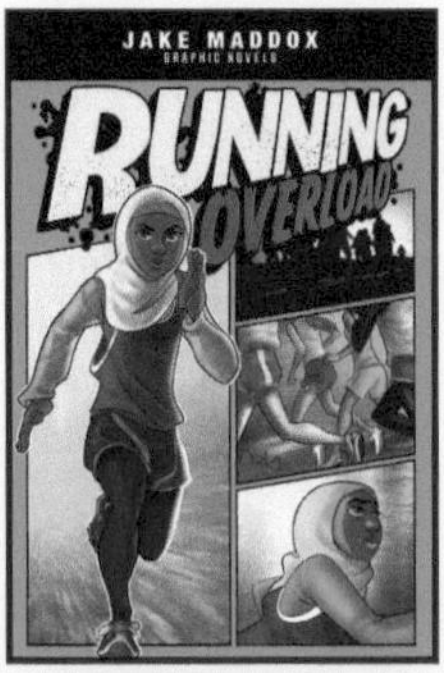
JAKE MADDOX
GRAPHIC NOVELS
RUNNING OVERLOAD

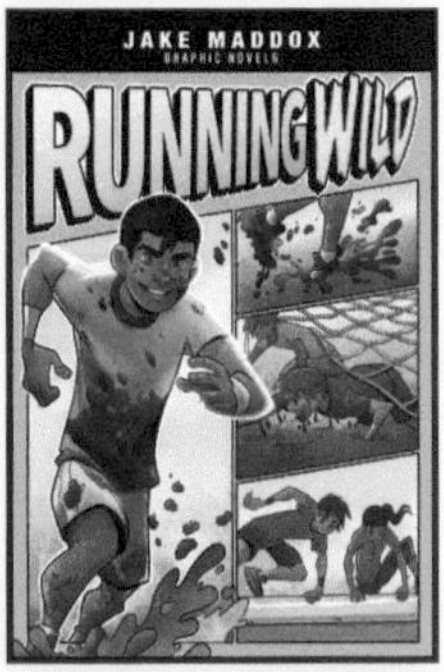
JAKE MADDOX
GRAPHIC NOVELS
RUNNING WILD

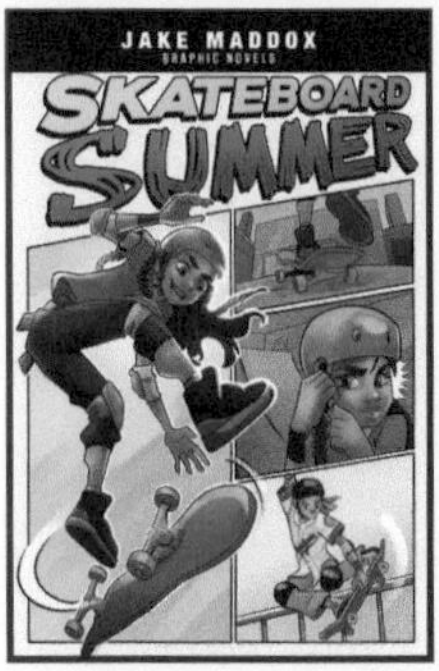
JAKE MADDOX
GRAPHIC NOVELS
SKATEBOARD SUMMER

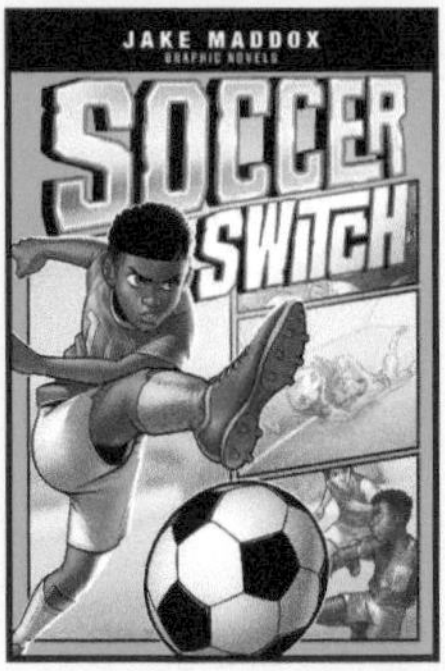
JAKE MADDOX
GRAPHIC NOVELS
SOCCER SWITCH

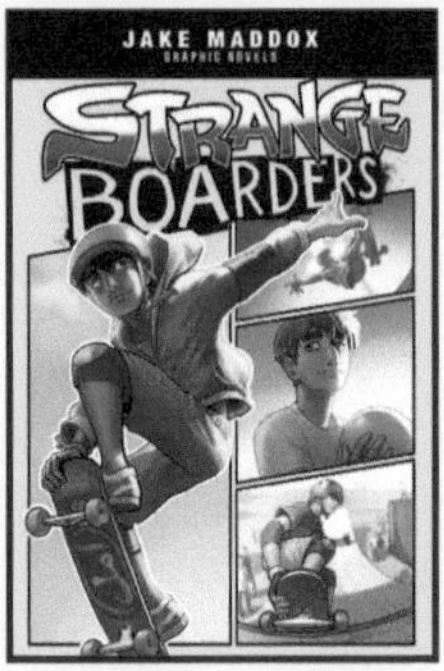
JAKE MADDOX
GRAPHIC NOVELS
STRANGE BOARDERS

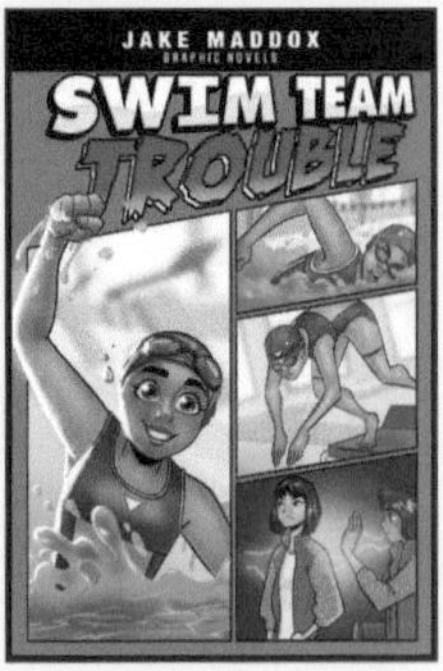
JAKE MADDOX
GRAPHIC NOVELS
SWIM TEAM TROUBLE